Nomi's Hiding Place

A Refugee Friend Story

Catherine Palmer

Lens&Pens Publishing LLC
Auburn WA

ISBN-10: 0692468226
ISBN-13: 978-0692468227

DEDICATION

For the women of the Refugee Sewing Society,
my inspiration and my joy.

Catherine Palmer

ACKNOWLEDGEMENTS

I'm grateful to so many. I thank the ladies and volunteers of the Refugee Sewing Society for their encouragement and love. I'm particularly grateful to Elizabeth Alier and Alawia Abaker for helping me understand the wars that have plagued Sudan and South Sudan. My husband, Tim Palmer, beautifully edits my manuscripts. Brian Bollinger, Steve Flesher, and Eric Anderson of Friends of Refugees provide undying support for all I do. My family, Harold and Phyllis Cummins, Libby Bennett, Geoffrey and Katharine Palmer, and Andrei Palmer hold me together through all the ups and downs of life. Skeeter Wilson, my publisher in this endeavor, has provided great assistance and advice.

Most important of all, I'm indebted to the gracious mercy and favor of the Lord Jesus Christ.

He will cover you with his feathers.
He will shelter you with his wings.
His faithful promises are your armor and protection.
Psalm 91:4 (NLT)

Catherine Palmer

CHAPTER ONE

At the sharp cry ringing out through the evening air, Nomi shivered. Holding her breath, she peered through a small hole in the mud wall of the storage house. Her eyes flicked back and forth as she searched the shadows for rebel soldiers streaming out of the forest and into her village. With flaming torches held high, they would aim their terrible guns at her beautiful home and the family inside.

And then, suddenly, she recognized the cry as her mother's voice.

"Nomi! Where is that girl?" Standing in the doorway of a large round house with a thatched grass roof, Mama shook her head. Again, she called into the warm evening air, "Nomi, the rice is cooked, and the stew is almost ready to eat! Where are you hiding now?"

As Mama gave up the search and stepped back into

their snug home, Nomi let out a shattered breath. No rebels, no guns, no torches, it had been only her mother calling. Mama never would have guessed that her youngest daughter was sitting on a heap of dried beans only a short distance away.

Nomi's family and friends all knew she loved to tuck herself into secret places. Sometimes high in trees. Sometimes behind fences or under market carts or near the river bank. And sometimes in a place so well protected only she and her best friend, Miriam, knew of it.

When her friends played a game of hiding and searching for each other, Nomi was always the last to be found. Often her brothers and sisters complained about looking for her to help with chores. As they sat around the cooking fire in the evening, one or the other of the twelve would frequently tell of a hopeless search for Nomi.

"Little Lamb," Nomi's father, Baba, often said gently, calling her by the special name he had given her. "I'm afraid that one day you'll hide, and you won't be able to find yourself."

Now in the faded light of the setting sun, Nomi giggled at the idea of such a silly thing. But she liked what Baba always reminded her. "The best place to hide, Nomi, is in the shelter of God's wings."

Imagining God's mighty wings covering her softly and keeping her safe, Nomi knelt in the dried beans and began to put away her treasures for the night – one of them more precious than all the others.

❖ ❖ ❖

Two years before, during the dry season when the northern people came south to trade, Nomi's best friend gave her a special gift. Miriam and Nomi were together only a few months a year, but they loved each other more than they loved any of their other friends. They were as close as sisters, they had decided. And much more fun.

One afternoon they were sharing a mango in their very secret best-friends-hiding-place. After they had sucked all the juicy pulp off the big mango seed, Miriam wiped her hands on a leaf and took a small wrapped bundle from beneath her long gown. "I want you to take this, Nomi," she said, her brown eyes serious. "In my religion, we're not allowed to own such things as this. It is *haram*, forbidden. But I couldn't leave it in the road where I found it."

Nomi took the gift and placed it in her lap. With great care she began to unfold the soft banana leaves Miriam had used as a wrapping.

"I'm afraid of it," Miriam whispered.

Nomi paused. Miriam was a strong girl with a round face, a loud voice, and a quick tongue. She wasn't afraid of anything. Or anyone. She had been known to take a stick and run after the boys who called Nomi "Goat Face." She had

3

thrown stones and scared away a pack of wild dogs threatening her family's sheep. Once she had been stung by a scorpion, and she didn't even scream.

❖ ❖ ❖

Now, as she hid in the storage barn, Nomi ran her hand over the face of the small doll Miriam had given her that day long ago. She was used to the doll's appearance. It was normal to her, even comforting, she thought, as she smoothed back the hair and tightened the fabric wrapped around the little shoulders.

But when the two friends first gazed together at the figure lying on the banana leaves, Nomi had felt a cold chill wash down her spine. The doll was missing its arms and legs. And it had white skin. Skin as white as the belly of a camel. As white as sugar in the market shops. It had hair the color of a ripe banana peel. And the lips? They were pink. Though the doll's blue eyes shone with tenderness, Nomi had agreed with Miriam. This thing looked terrifying.

Nomi, Miriam, and everyone else in the village had heard that white men and women lived in the big cities of Africa. They were good people, it was well known, because they sent doctors to heal wounds, mosquito nets to fight sickness, and airplanes to drop bags of food onto the ground of South Sudan. Miriam claimed to have seen hundreds of white people in Khartoum and the other cities her people

4

visited to do their trading. But the doll, with bleached white skin and staring blue eyes, was enough to scare Miriam and all the children in Nomi's village.

"What do you think?" Miriam had asked Nomi that warm afternoon. "Should I take it back to the road and let my baba's truck run over it?"

"Never," Nomi said. "She is ugly, but I will love this girl child. I'll take care of her as though she's a real baby. And every time I see her, I will remember my best friend."

Miriam was pleased, and Nomi took the doll home to show her family.

❖ ❖ ❖

As Nomi expected, everyone jumped backward in shock when she showed them Miriam's gift. But gradually, they grew accustomed to seeing it tied to her back, like a real baby. Nomi's favorite brother carved wooden legs and arms for the doll. He instructed his sister to be a good mother and keep her child's skin clean and well oiled. He found a scrap of pink flowered fabric in the trash on his way to school and gave it to Nomi.

"Here, Little Lamb," Andrau said as he handed her the cloth. "Wrap your daughter in this and give her a good name. Call her Esther, like the queen in the Bible. Your child is ugly, but Queen Esther was beautiful. You know, when ugly girls grow up, they always turn out to be as pretty as queens."

Now Nomi smiled at the memory. She felt sure her brother was telling her that one day *she* would be a beautiful woman. Andrau had heard the children in the village teasing Nomi because she had a long, thin face and a grin that went from ear to ear.

"Your father calls you Little Lamb," the boys taunted her, "but you have the face of a goat! Goat face, goat face!"

They often mocked Nomi until she ran away and hid, wiping away hot tears of shame. Andrau had given his sister a hug and planted a big kiss on Esther's plastic forehead.

❖❖❖

Now, tucked away in the storage barn while the sun dipped low in the sky, Nomi surveyed her family's large compound near the center of the village. Hard-packed earth formed a floor on which sat her father's house, three storage barns, the houses of her two oldest brothers and their wives and children, the *luak* - their large house for cattle, and the two pens rimmed with thorn brush where the family's goats and sheep slept safely through the night. It was a good home, and soon the open area would be filled with people gathering to eat around the cooking fire.

Shifting, she heard dried beans scatter beneath her. "Did you see what Andrau brought home today?" she whispered to her doll. "Guinea fowl. Two of them! Mama cooked them while we were milking the sheep and putting them in the pen. You sleep here, my baby, and I'll take you with me to fetch water tomorrow morning."

Nomi scooped out a hollow place in the bean pile, placed Esther into it, and covered her with more beans until only her strange blue eyes showed in the light coming through the peephole.

CHAPTER TWO

"Rebels burned twelve houses across the river," Andrau informed his father as he picked up a handful of cornmeal mush from the large round pot around which his family ate their meals. "The whole village is gone. There's nothing left but a few cooking stones. They stole all the goats and cattle, too."

"Hush, boy!" Nomi's father admonished him. "Don't talk of such things while we eat. The girls will become afraid."

"Baba, your youngest daughter is Nomi, and she's twelve years old already," Andrau continued. "In two or three years, you'll be getting her a husband. She needs to understand about the rebels, or she won't know what to do when they come here."

"Andrau, please stop." Mama put her hand on her son's arm. "You know Nomi goes to school and that means she won't marry until she's much older. Let her be a child now, and keep her free from these fears. Besides, the rebels would never come to our village."

"They would, Mama," he argued. "They will!"

"For what? We're poor people with only a few cattle and goats. Our sheep are so thin they're not worth eating." Mama pushed a mound of mush toward Grandmother, who never seemed to eat enough these days. "If they burned our storage house, what would we lose? A few beans!"

"The heart of man is evil," Grandmother said, looking around at her family in the dim light of the hut. "But God is good. We are His people, the sheep of His grasslands."

Andrau clamped his mouth shut. Nomi knew he would never dare to argue with his grandmother. Grandmother knew everything, or at least all the children thought so. No matter what happened in the village – a baby was born, an old man died, a cow escaped, a new school opened – Grandmother always spoke the right words about it. God's words.

Though Nomi's greatest treasure was her blue-eyed, yellow-haired Esther, Grandmother owned something much more valuable – a Bible. Her holy book lay wrapped in many layers of newspaper on a stool beside her bed, and she held it close to her heart in the morning when she said her prayers.

The Bible had been given to Grandmother years ago by a man who told her that in it were written all the words of

God. All of them! These words were in English, which meant that neither Grandmother nor any of the other adults in the village could read them. But they held great power all the same.

The man who gave Grandmother the Bible had taught everyone those words of God. He was a doctor who had passed through the village with medicine and Bibles when she was a girl. He stayed only a few days, but when he told the people about God – and about Jesus, who had defeated death by dying and then coming alive again – everyone believed what he said. Everyone from the oldest man to the smallest child knew the message was true.

Sometimes in the evenings, Grandmother would unwrap the newspapers and give the Bible to Andrau to read, because he knew a little bit of English and could explain God's words to everyone using their clan's language. The more Andrau read, the more the people believed what the doctor had told Grandmother about Jesus.

"God is good," Nomi repeated her grandmother's words that evening, "and I don't believe He'll let the rebels come to our village. He will protect us with His wings. I'm not afraid of anyone."

"Well, you're stupid, then," an older brother, Luke, snapped at her. He was fifteen and full of himself. He had the loudest voice of anyone in the family, and now he turned it on Nomi. "The rebels have big guns, and they go anywhere they want, and they burn down villages and kill all the people. Maybe God loves us, but not enough to save us from the rebels."

"Yes, He does!" Nomi shot back. "They won't kill me. I'm going to hide beneath God's wings."

"Where are those wings, Nomi? Have you seen them?" Luke was angry now. "In school, we studied about the wars all over the world in every country in every year of the history of this earth. People fight and kill each other, and God doesn't protect any of them."

"Maybe they don't believe in Him, Luke," she retorted. "Have you thought about that?"

"I've thought about it, and I don't believe in Him either!" Luke glared at his family seated in a circle around the food. "My friend, John – my best friend at school – he lived in the village Andrau told us about, the one to the south of us across the river. Our teacher said that last week the rebels burned down John's house and took away his mother and all of his sisters, and they shot John and his father and every one of his brothers."

Tears spilled down Luke's cheeks. He wiped them away with a fist. "Our teacher told us that John is in a hospital in Juba, but all his brothers and his father died. All of them are dead!" he shouted, "All of them!"

"Enough, Luke!" Baba said firmly. "Stop talking. Go

to the water pot and bring a bowl of water for your family to drink. A full bowl. Enough for everyone."

Luke scrambled to his feet. "One day, I am going to get a gun myself, and I'm going to kill rebels," he hollered as he stalked away. "I'll kill as many as I can before they kill me!"

"Luke!" Baba began to rise from the floor, but his son scampered away from the firelight and into the darkness.

Nomi could hear her little brothers softly whimpering. The baby had begun to cry, and Mama was jiggling him up and down to soothe him.

Baba looked around at his family. "Luke is right that God doesn't always protect His people," he said. "But Grandmother is right, too. God does protect them many times. One way is by putting His people into families with strong fathers and strapping big brothers. And that is how He will keep us safe."

"Baba speaks the truth," Andrau announced. "We have our slings and our clubs and our spears, and we're all very smart and powerful. We'll protect this family, so stop crying, little ones."

Nomi felt a flicker of warmth begin to melt the icy fear that had crept through her at Luke's words. "Yes, that's true," she affirmed for the smaller children. "Baba, and Andrau, and the big boys will protect us. God made that good plan for our family."

"God always has a good plan for us," Mama agreed. "Children, don't be afraid. Your baba and your brothers will keep you safe." She glanced up as Luke returned to the fire with a bowl of water. "We'll be safe without carrying guns. No guns for my family."

Luke's jaw was set, the small muscles twitching. Nomi knew that look very well. In the moments he was away collecting water, her brother had made up his mind to do something. Something that was not good.

Grandmother took a long drink from the bowl before passing it to Mama. She cleared her throat. "Once, long ago, there lived a man and a woman," she began. Nomi and her brothers and sisters quickly scooted closer to their grandmother. They all knew this tale by heart, and they loved it.

"God gave this man and woman a rich farm full of mango trees, banana trees, and coconut palms. They had one hundred fat cows and fifty brown goats. Monkeys never stole the bananas, and coconuts never fell on anyone's head. God told them to eat from all the trees except the one that bore a fruit they had never tasted. All was well until one day, a snake slithered out from the banana grove."

At this, one of Nomi's sisters gave a little squeak, but everyone shushed her so Grandmother could continue.

"The snake told the woman to eat the fruit she had

never tasted. The woman said, 'Snake, God ordered my husband and me not to eat that fruit.' But Snake told her it was delicious, and it would make her grow very smart. So what do you think she did?"

"She ate it!" Nomi shouted along with her siblings.

"Yes, she ate it. And then she gave the fruit to her husband, and he ate it, too."

"Oh, no!" a tiny brother cried out.

"God saw what they had done," Grandmother continued. "And He was very angry. He threw them out of their beautiful farm, and made them live among thorn bushes where there was no water to drink. That's because they disobeyed Him."

"That's a good punishment," Nomi declared. "You should not disobey God."

"Little Lamb is correct," Baba said gently. Nomi beamed that her father had acknowledged her statement.

"Yes, but then something even worse happened." Grandmother's voice dropped, and everyone leaned closer. "The man and the woman had two children, both of them boys. The boys always gave gifts to God so He would be pleased with them. Like all strong warriors, God wanted meat – good meat with lots of fat on it to drip into the fire and make the smoke smell wonderful. One day, the two boys brought gifts to God. The older one brought the best meat of his largest, fattest sheep. But the younger brother brought a bowl of cooked beans."

"Nooo!" the children cried out. Everyone knew beans made a terrible gift. There was nothing special about beans. Even the poorest people had beans to eat, because they could be grown – or stolen – anywhere.

"Of course, God was delighted with the fat meat," Grandmother told them, "but He didn't like the beans at all. This made the younger brother so angry that he hit his older brother with a rock and killed him. Now, why do you think that boy did such a bad thing? It was because his father and mother, before him, had done a bad thing. That boy did wrong, because his parents did wrong. And do you know what happened after that? The boy had children, and they did bad things, too. So did his grandchildren and their children. That's how evil came into the world, and that, my dearest Luke, is why the rebels shot your friend and his family."

Luke looked down at the fire as his grandmother spoke her final words. "If people were good, as God intended them to be, the whole world would be full of fat cows and goats, swift rivers, and mango trees. Everyone would be safe. But God always lets people choose. Sometimes, like that brother who gave a gift of beans, they choose to be bad, and they kill their brothers, even the ones God loves the most."

As Grandmother finished her story, Mama covered the

fire with a pot so it would go to sleep.

Later that night as Nomi and her sisters lay in the girls' sleeping hut near the main house, she listened to the sounds of the dark night outside – crickets singing to their wives, bush babies crying forlornly, birds calling out good-night, good-night. If the rebels came, she decided as sleep drifted over her family, she would be like the brother who gave God meat. She would help the men of her family keep the others safe, and she knew exactly how she would do that. She had a plan.

CHAPTER THREE

At school the next day, Nomi's plan slipped into the back of her mind. As always, she played at jumping rope with her friends, the boys chased her and called her Goat Face, and the teachers led their students in reciting lessons and singing educational songs. The arguments and harsh words spoken around her family's evening meal faded as Nomi worked hard to learn her lessons.

School subjects were taught from tattered textbooks, most of them smelling of kerosene where teachers from many years past had studied into the night. The supply of chalk gave out, as it always did when traders from the north left the southern towns and villages to go in search of wares. Teachers then wrote on their smooth boards with charcoal. Charcoal was harder to read, Nomi knew, but every child longed to learn and did their best to copy the writing into their school notebooks.

Nomi kept her notebook clean by wrapping it in brown paper that Miriam brought as a gift one day. Miriam didn't get to go to school, as Nomi did, but she wanted to learn. Sometimes they went to their very-secret-best-friends-hiding-place and pretended that the grassy space amid a ring of huge stones was a schoolroom. Nomi was always the teacher, of course. Miriam listened intently when her friend taught the alphabet and recited the few English words she knew.

"I am a boy," Miriam said one day as she stood beside the rock that represented her desk. "My name is Miriam, and i am a boy."

This sent Nomi into gales of laughter. "I am a girl," she corrected her friend. "I am a girl, not a boy."

Miriam glowered for a moment, because she hated to be wrong. Then the two friends chanted the correct words again and again until they had made them into a song they sang every time they saw each other.

Nomi taught Miriam how to count and add numbers. She explained about America, a far-off land where every person had plenty of food to eat and beautiful clothes, where no one walked without shoes, and where, if you touched the wall of your house, water would suddenly stream out. She told Miriam that all the white people in the world lived in America – unless they were visiting the big cities of South Sudan.

School ended and all the children raced home to help with chores. Girls paired up over a large wooden pot filled with white corn kernels. Holding onto a tall pole together, they pounded the corn into flour. Some traveled to the river in groups, clay jars balanced on their heads. After filling their jars, they helped each other return the vessels to their heads for the long walk back to the village. The boys scampered off to tend the cows, goats, and sheep their families owned. Occasionally, some of the lucky ones went into the forest with their fathers and older brothers to shoot birds or wild game for dinner.

As Nomi pounded cornmeal, she practiced her alphabet and numbers, her English words, or the songs her teachers taught her. But more and more these days, she thought about the rebel soldiers with their big guns. Sometimes she thought she saw someone moving among the banana trees, and she stiffened for a moment.

"What's wrong with you, girl?" her older sister snapped one afternoon. Dorcas, at thirteen, claimed that her advanced age gave her superiority over Nomi. "Three times today you've stopped pounding and nearly made me tip over the cornmeal! If you do it again, I'm going to tell Mama, and then what? She'll tell Baba, and you'll be in big trouble!"

"I'm sorry, Dorcas, but I think someone's hiding in the banana trees. Just look over there!"

Dorcas caught her breath and peered into the dense thicket of green trunks and leaves. "Where?" she whispered. "Where is he?"

"I don't know. He keeps moving around. But maybe it's not —"

"Let's go tell Andrau!"

"No, wait!" Nomi took a deep breath, trying to calm her heart. "It might have been the wind. There's a little breeze. See it ruffling the leaves of that guava tree?"

"I don't care about wind. I'm not staying here to get shot dead by rebel soldiers!"

Dorcas dropped the pounding pole, grabbed her skirts, and raced toward the house. As she fled, the pot tipped over and cornmeal spilled across the hard dirt floor of their compound. With a squeak, Nomi dropped to her knees and tried to scoop it up. Their dinner wouldn't be fit to eat. The corn cakes would taste of dust and stones. Giving up quickly, she too ran to the house.

"We saw a rebel," Dorcas was sobbing, as she grabbed her mother's arm. "Nomi saw him in the bananas! Where is Baba? Where's Andrau?"

"They're with the cows," Mama said. "Nomi, thank God you're here. How many soldiers did you see?"

"I'm not sure —"

"Grab the babies outside, Nomi." Mama cut her off. "And shut the door behind you! Everyone under the beds!"

Nomi scooped up her two little brothers and scampered back into the house. Everyone slid beneath the low beds, Nomi's hand clapped over one of the boys' mouth and Dorcas's over the other. Mama began to murmur a prayer. Grandmother, wedged in beside Nomi, was breathing hard. She had slid under the beds along with the rest of the children who had been in the house.

But some were missing, Nomi realized. Where was Luke? Oh, if he had truly gotten a gun, he might be able to save them! What about the older sisters and brothers? Where were they? Hiding beneath the beds was a terrible plan! The soldiers would look there first, and then everyone would be dragged out into the open and shot. What would it feel like to have a bullet tear into your chest, Nomi thought frantically. Tears welled in her eyes, but she knew she mustn't make a sound.

As terrible minutes gathered one upon another, those under the bed grew still. Some of the children actually fell asleep, but others whimpered and wiggled and refused to be calmed. Nomi, heart beating like a drum, realized suddenly how hungry she was after the long school day, and how thirsty. She listened for the sound of gunfire. But what did guns sound like? Stones falling on each other? Someone clapping? An elephant trumpeting? Cattle hoofs thundering down to the river? She couldn't imagine.

"Oh, great and strong God of Grandmother's Bible, please protect us under Your wings!" she prayed. "Please keep my family safe!"

Baba and the big brothers would be arriving soon. They'd all be killed! But how could Baba die? He was so strong, and he smiled so warmly at her. It was impossible to think of life without Baba.

Suddenly voices rang out across the clearing. "Where are they?" someone shouted. "I don't see anyone!"

Nomi squeezed her eyes shut and tried not to cry.

"Andrau, do you see anyone near the barns?" It was Baba's voice! Baba and her brothers were home, and the rebel soldiers had left the compound. Or never had been there at all.

"Oh, thank God!" Mama wiggled out from under the bed, and her children tumbled after her. She threw open the door and ran to her husband. "The rebels came," she cried, "but we hid under the beds for hours and finally they went away!"

"Rebels?" Baba stiffened. "Did they come into the house? Did they burn anything or steal a goat? I see no sign of rebels here. Where were they, my wife?"

"Perhaps they didn't actually come into the compound," Mama told him. "But Dorcas said Nomi saw them in the banana thicket."

"Yes, she did it!" Dorcas exclaimed, her long arm stretched out and her finger pointed at Nomi. "She told me the rebel soldiers were in the banana trees. It's all her fault!"

All eyes turned on Nomi. For a moment, she hung speechless, quaking before her father and all his strong sons.

"Nomi?" Baba glowered at her. "Did you see men in the bananas?"

"I thought I heard them, Baba," she whispered. "There were shadows. Black shadows moving in the bananas. But it might have been wind making the green stalks shiver. Maybe it was a snake. Maybe . . . I'm afraid that maybe there were no soldiers at all."

She squeezed her eyes shut and waited for her father's wrath to descend on her.

"You see?" Baba shouted. "Andrau? Luke? Do you see what you've done with all your stories? You've terrified Mama and the girls and babies. This whole family is seeing soldiers everywhere. There will be no more tales of rebel soldiers or burning villages in my compound! Do you understand me?"

The boys nodded, shuffling their feet and looking away in shame. "Yes, Baba. Yes, sir."

"Now where is the food, my wife?" Baba demanded. "Everyone is hungry and tired, and I'm finished with all this foolishness."

Mama gaped at the cold firestones where no fire danced beneath cooking pots bubbling with stew. Nomi shifted her eyes to the fallen pounding pot and the cornmeal spilled across the dirt. She wished she could crawl into the barn and hide beneath the beans.

Mama scowled at her. "We will be eating late, my husband. Nomi, go and collect some bananas for your family. And try not to imagine rebel soldiers in the bushes."

CHAPTER FOUR

After the incident of the soldiers in the banana trees – or rather the soldiers *not* in the banana trees – Nomi's family returned to their normal life. At least it seemed that way with the girls watching babies, fetching water and pounding cornmeal, the boys tending the goats and cattle, and Grandmother telling stories by the fire at night.

But Nomi didn't feel normal at all. She had seen what fear could do, and she'd had plenty of time under the bed to think about her family's future.

The soldiers, Andrau told them, had now moved to the west and were raiding villages there. He said they shouldn't become too relaxed, though. At any time, the attackers could return to their area. Everyone ought to keep a watch for strangers, and all should report news about the fighting to him or Baba.

"Andrau, I've made a plan for us," Nomi told her big brother one day as they walked toward the school. "It's a good plan, a way for us to escape when the rebels come back."

"Leave the planning to the men, my sister," Andrau said. "You're just a little girl. You shouldn't even be thinking about these things."

"So the men have a plan? Does Luke own a gun now?"

Andrau cut her a glance. "Did you hear what Mama said about guns? Nomi, you must not think about such things."

"How can I not think about soldiers raiding our compound? I know they're not far away."

"Look what happened the last time you thought about them. You started seeing rebels in the banana trees!"

Nomi fell silent, embarrassment creeping over her again. When Dorcas had blabbered the news at school, the boys teased her all the more. "Goat Face, Goat Face," they yelled at her. "Look out behind you! There's a rebel just there, in the shadows!"

She wondered if they would still be shouting at her when she was an old grandmother with sons and daughters and lots of grandchildren. In her mind, she pictured some of the boys running past her house and shouting, "Goat Face! How are you today, Goat Face?"

"Your imagination is too strong," Andrau was saying, and Nomi's cheeks grew hot as she realized her most recent thoughts affirmed her brother's statement.

"Baba and the men of our family are indeed making plans," Andrau told her. "We're the strong and wise ones. The men should take responsibility for the family."

"The men? Where were you when we thought the rebels had come? You were all away from the compound doing your strong, wise things. It was just us – the women and the babies – left to face the enemy."

"You're not a woman," Andrau retorted.

"If I didn't go to school, I'd be getting married in two or three years. I'm enough of a woman to think about protecting my family."

"Just stop thinking so much, Nomi. We'll take care of you."

Nomi fumed. They were almost at the school, and she hadn't been able to convince her brother of anything. "Don't you want to know my plan?" she asked. "It's a really good one."

He shot her another glance, his eyebrows drawn together. "Drop the subject, sister. I have more important things to think about."

As he loped off, Nomi saw the "more important thing" her brother was after. Standing under a mango tree, Ruth stood chewing on sugar cane and laughing with her girlfriends. Everyone knew Ruth was the most beautiful young woman in the whole village. Every boy of marriageable age was hoping to catch her eye. Several of them had already gone to her father, asking for her hand in marriage. So far, Ruth's father had turned them all away.

With a sigh, Nomi looked down at the packed red soil of the open area around the school. No one listened to her, and no one would ever think of marrying her. She wasn't worth the pile of beans in the storage room where her doll slept at night.

"Good morning, Goat Face!" several of the boys shouted as they galloped past her, kicking their ragged ball toward the goal. She halted, hands on her hip, trying to think of a good retort.

"Good morning, Little Lamb," a low voice said, as the speaker trotted after the others with the ball.

Little Lamb? Nomi lifted her head in surprise. As her eyes followed him, she saw it was Peter smiling at her as he headed into the crowd of boys. Peter was not the best looking boy in the school or the quickest at football, but he was definitely the smartest. He won every spelling and math contest, and he always collected the most prizes at the end of every term. Peter was the leader of his house at school, and this gave him power over the other, stronger boys.

Nomi paused, holding her hand over her eyes against the rising sun. Peter? she thought. She watched him muscle his way to the ball and felt a strange warmth flood through her heart. Maybe one of the boys didn't think of her as ugly as a goat. Maybe that boy was Peter.

❖❖❖

The best news in the world greeted Nomi that afternoon as she descended the steps of the school.

"Hello, Nomi!" the familiar voice rang out across the clearing. A small, robed figure danced and waved at her from behind the school fence.

Nomi laughed. "Miriam! You're back!"

Nomi's best friend was skirting the fence now, pushing past the other children. "We're back! We came down from Khartoum and arrived last night!"

Miriam looked somehow different than Nomi remembered as they raced toward each other.

"You're wearing hijab!" She took Miriam's hands and spun her around. The hijab, a colorful hood that stretched over Miriam's head and around her plump cheeks, billowed in the early evening breeze. "It's beautiful! You look like a real woman now!"

Miriam giggled. "My mama said I could start wearing hijab, and my big sister gave me one of hers. And then my baba bought me this one while we were in Khartoum. So I have two, and now I wear them all the time!"

"I'm so happy to see you," Nomi said, giving her a

warm hug. "I have so much to tell!"

"And I have a terrible secret to tell you." Miriam could never keep quiet about secrets. "You'll never guess the disaster that has happened. You know Abdul, that tall boy who I hate with my whole heart? Last month, he asked baba if he could marry me."

"No! Not Abdul!" Nomi exclaimed in horror. "Surely your baba said no."

The two girls were headed arm-in-arm toward their most secret hiding place. Neither had said a word about where they would go, but it was their tradition to meet in the little clearing amid the boulders just after Nomi's school rang the last bell of the day. No one else could hear their secrets there, and they would be completely hidden from prying eyes.

"You can't stand Abdul!" Nomi continued. "He's always throwing pebbles at you, and he loves to put his foot in your path and make you trip. I've never even met him, and I hate him as much as you do."

"Well, he doesn't hate me, and now I have to be his wife."

"Oh, Miriam." Nomi shook her head. "How can it be? He's so mean to you. He makes your life miserable."

"And he's going to make it even more miserable. He told me he liked me, and everything he did to me was because he loved to see me getting angry. Can you imagine that? A husband who wants to make his wife angry! What will my life be?"

Nomi realized that Miriam was dabbing her eyes with the hem of her hijab. Helping each other, they clambered over the large stones that nearly blocked the entrance to their hideaway. When they were seated in the cool shadows, Miriam took a small packet of cookies from under her robe. She unwrapped the newspapers around the treat, and as the two girls ate, they discussed this horrible news.

"Miriam, isn't Abdul twenty years old?" Nomi asked.

"He's twenty-one."

"And you're only eleven."

"Mama says she thinks I'm twelve by now." Miriam sighed. "It's the way of my religion, you know. I can't go to school or have any hope of a life different from the one my mother and grandmother had. I don't mind. And really, you know, Abdul isn't so bad a choice."

"But you hate him!"

"His family is wealthy. They have more cows than anyone in our clan, and when we're trading in Khartoum, they live in a big house with a stone floor and many windows. Abdul told me they have a car, but I think he's lying about that."

"I'm sure he is. One the very richest people own cars. That's the way it is."

"Either way, I'll live in that fine house and have

servants to bring my food and wash my clothes."

Nomi gaped at her friend. "Miriam, I think you want to marry Abdul."

"Well . . ." Miriam shrugged. "Allah, my god, does whatever he wants with us, and we can't change anything. We're at his mercy. If I have 15 children, that is the will of Allah. If I learn to drive a car, that's his will, too."

"And if your husband beats you because he loves to make you angry? Is that the will of your god?"

"Yes, it is." Miriam hung her head for a moment. "There's nothing I can do to change the will of Allah."

"That's not the way of my God," Nomi said. "He listens to us when we pray. He loves us and wants the best for us. He hides us under His big wings."

At this, Miriam giggled. "Is your God a rooster or maybe a big hen?"

Nomi sighed. "Miriam, I don't know everything about God, but I do know He's not a chicken. And I know He loves me. He wants the best for me, and so does my baba." Nomi paused for a moment, thinking about Peter and his smile. "I don't believe they would marry me to a bad man."

Miriam wiped crumbs from her lips. "You'll see, Nomi. When the time comes, your father will marry you to the man who brings the most wealth and power to your family. That's what he'll do."

At that, they stood and prepared to part to their respective homes to pound cornmeal, fetch water, and watch babies. On an impulse, Nomi gave her friend a warm hug. "I love you Miriam," she said. "And I hope you'll remember me when you live in your big house in Khartoum."

"Of course I will!" Miriam exclaimed. "You're my best friend. My best friend in all the world."

CHAPTER FIVE

Nomi held her head high as she walked to church with her family on a Sunday afternoon. Nearby villages took turns worshiping in the small building, and 3 p.m. was their allotted time. She wore her clean church uniform, a pleated blue dress and matching sweater. These were her very nicest clothes, and like most of the other children in her village, Nomi was happy to wear the uniform as an important tradition for children in the South Sudanese churches. Dorcas had given her a pair of sandals which were too big but bright blue and extremely beautiful. Best of all, Grandmother had chosen Nomi to carry the precious Bible.

"I saw you talking with that friend of yours, that girl, Miriam, who travels down here with the traders," Dorcas said, stepping to Nomi's side as they walked. "You shouldn't even say hello to those people, you know. They have the same religion as the rebel soldiers, and that's why they're killing us. They hate us because of what we believe about God."

"That's not the reason," Nomi retorted. "They want to take over our land and our government. That's why they raid our villages."

"Hah! You're not as smart as you think, sister. The trouble is religion. I've seen you and your friend sneaking away together after school. You'd better make sure Baba doesn't find out about it, or you'll be in big trouble."

"I'm not afraid for people to see us. I like Miriam. She's been my friend since we were very young, and she's certainly nothing like the rebel soldiers."

"But what about that man she's going to marry? That Abdul with the big nose? How do you know where he spends his day? Maybe he goes raiding while she's at the market with her baba. They're selling oil and sugar while Abdul is off killing people and burning villages."

"Stop talking like that!" Nomi hissed. "How do you know about Abdul anyway?"

"People talk, you know. Nothing's secret in this village. When my friends and I go down to the market to buy sweets, we chat with the sellers. That's how we learn the news."

"Then you're a gossip! You shouldn't go around spreading rumors you don't even know are true."

"So it's not true? Miriam is not the same religion as the rebels, and she's not going to marry Abdul Big Nose?" Dorcas laughed. "I can see in your eyes it's all true. That's the trouble with having a goat face – everyone can see exactly what you're thinking."

"I hate you, Dorcas!" Nomi spat. "You're cruel, and you don't care about anyone but yourself. Here, take your stupid shoes!"

She kicked off the beautiful blue sandals and ran

barefooted to the church door. As she sat with the others of her village for the three or four hours their worship usually lasted, Nomi couldn't think about anything but her horrible sister. Dorcas was the worst sister in the world. Why had God put someone so spiteful into her family?

It's true that Miriam believed a different way about God, but she was much nicer than Dorcas. Nomi couldn't imagine Miriam's father marrying his youngest daughter to one of those rebel soldiers. He was a fat old man with a long white beard and three wives and too many children to count. He sold oil in large jerry cans and big blocks of sugar wrapped in newspaper. Sometimes he had rice, which tasted so much better than cornmeal.

Whenever Nomi was allowed to go down to the shops, Miriam's father always gave her a lump of sugar to suck on and several coins to carry in her pocket. Like Miriam, he made Nomi laugh by teasing her and telling funny stories. One time he gave her a beautiful wooden comb, and another time he handed her a metal bracelet with engravings of birds all around it. She thought he was a wonderful baba, even though he was not her baba. And her baba was better than all the other babas God had ever made.

After the church worshipers had eaten a meal together, Nomi set out for home with her family. Still thinking about the things that hateful Dorcas had accused her of, she decided to ask Andrau her questions.

"Brother," she said, moving to his side, "are the rebel soldiers killing us because of religion?"

"Didn't I tell you not to think about such things anymore?" he admonished her. He looked down and let out a sigh. "Yes, it is religion. But it's also the rich land we own, and the government that rules our country, and probably other things we don't even know."

"Do you believe the Khartoum traders help the rebels? Do they tell them secrets about us? Are the traders as bad as that?"

"Nomi, no one but God knows what's in the heart of a man. You should –"

A thunderous boom split open the air around them. Dirt flew up into Nomi's face and filled her mouth. She could see nothing through the thick dust. And then another boom thundered a short distance away. She hung motionless in shock. Before she could move, Andrau caught her by the arm.

"Run, Nomi! Run to the compound! It's the rebels!" he shouted at her.

A wash of chills spilled down Nomi's spine. She grabbed a little brother, set him on her hip and raced for the compound. She spotted Grandmother through the flying dust and screamed at her to hurry. Her mother was running with the baby and the other boy. The rest of the brothers and sisters sprinted toward the cluster of huts.

As Nomi rounded the fence and raced through the gate, she glanced over her shoulder. Dorcas hobbled far behind the rest of them, limping. Her face was contorted with pain. Bright red blood stained her leg.

"Dorcas!" she shouted. "Run! Run!"

"I can't!" Dorcas screamed back. "A bullet hit me! In my leg!"

A bullet? Nomi's fuzzy brain couldn't make sense of it. She reached the house and practically threw her little brother through the front door into one of the big sisters' arms. Then she swung around and raced back to Dorcas.

"Come on!" she shouted as booms filled the clearing. "Put your arm around my shoulders."

Her heart hammering, Nomi dragged her sister toward the house. Shouts and screams filled the air, and now came the sound of gunfire.

Ak-ak-ak-ak! Ak-ak-ak-ak! Ak-ak-ak-ak!

Bullets hit the ground near Nomi's feet as she and Dorcas plunged into the darkness of their house. As she stood gasping for air, Nomi immediately realized their danger.

"We're trapped!" she shouted over the uproar. "We're trapped inside this house! Baba! Andrau! We can't stay here!"

She searched through the crowded mass of brothers and sisters. Where were the big boys? Where was Baba? The house was filled with crying babies. Someone vomited. The putrid smell filled the hot air. Nomi thought she might faint. Several children were trying to slide under the beds. Dorcas lay writhing, moaning on the floor. Somebody was screaming – a single, high-pitched howl that made it impossible to think.

But Nomi did think. For a brief second, she thought clearly about her family stuffed inside their house. Bullets. Mortar shells. Fire. They didn't stand a chance. She spotted her mother, lunged forward, and grabbed her arm.

"Mama, I know a safe place in the forest!" she cried, recalling the plan she had formed not long ago. "No one can find us there. Tell the others to follow me."

"But we should hide here! We should wait for your baba!"

"No, Mama. We can't stay here. This house is a trap. If we don't leave now, they'll enter the compound, and it will be too late to save ourselves!"

Her mother fell silent for a moment, her eyes taking in the chaos.

"Follow Nomi!" she shouted at the children, her voice ringing through the house. "Everyone follow Nomi. Make sure we have the babies. Leave no one behind!"

Nomi paused beside the closed door for a moment, listening. Suddenly, it fell quiet outside, just an instant of silence. She threw open the door, raced around the house, and fled into the forest. Her feet stumbled over vines and roots. Thorns caught at her legs. The shooting started again.

Ak-ak-ak-ak! Ak-ak-ak-ak! Ak-ak-ak-ak! Boom! Boom! Ak-ak-ak-ak!

Nomi glanced behind her. One of the little boys had managed to keep close to her, so she scooped him up and kept running. She could see no one else in the dense undergrowth. Were they lost? Had they been captured – or shot? Tears swam in her eyes and tumbled down her cheeks as she traced her way through the forest toward the boulders by the stream.

"Nomi!"

It was one of the big brothers, catching up to her. "Where are you taking us? The rebels are right behind!"

"Just come! Follow me!"

At the right place, she plunged out of the trees and made for the pile of large stones where she and Miriam always played.

"In there!" she told her brother. "Just climb over the boulders as I do!"

Breathing hard, she set down her little brother and hurried him along as she clambered over the familiar rocks. Risking another glance behind, she saw that her family was with her. There was Mama, Dorcas, the babies, many of the others. She didn't have time to count.

Taking a breath, she dropped down into the grassy area

where she and Miriam had spent countless hours. She pushed her little brother toward the back of the clearing and helped the others over the stones and into the hiding place.

"Where's Grandmother?" she whispered to the older sister who was helping Dorcas over the stones. "Have you seen her?"

"She's just there! Look!"

Nomi spotted Grandmother scrambling up the rocks, and then she saw Andrau! And there was Baba! "Oh, thank you, God," Nomi breathed out. "Thank you for saving my family!"

In moments, everyone was tucked down in the cleft of the rocks, hidden by the large boulders and the clumps of grass that grew among them. Nomi tried to count, but she couldn't stop the tears of relief that blurred her vision and slid down her cheeks.

And then Mama squealed, "Luke! Where is Luke!"

Baba put his hand over her mouth and held her tightly. "He's safe. I'm sure of it!"

"But where?" She tried to shake free, but Baba hushed her. "Quiet, wife. They are near. I can hear them."

Nomi lifted her head just far enough to scan the forest. Luke was not to be seen, but a large plume of smoke drifted up from the place where the family compound stood. The storage huts! The house! The *kornuk*, where the children ate their meals! Even the shady *rakuba*, where everyone played. They would all burn to the ground. All the corn and beans, all the beds and blankets, and oil and sugar . . . and her doll. Nomi had left Esther that morning, sleeping in the storage barn.

She propped her arms on her bent knees, laid her forehead down, and let the tears flow. Even as she cried, she trembled with fear. What to do if they were discovered? But no, this place was perfectly safe. She and Miriam had hidden here for years with no one suspecting a thing.

"Oh, God," she prayed in silence. Please keep my family safe! Hide us under your wings!"

CHAPTER SIX

Two rebel soldiers came out of the forest only moments after the last of the family had tumbled down into the clearing among the big rocks. The men searched the riverbank, up and down, back and forth. Nomi heard them shouting at each other.

"Do you see anyone?"

"No. Those filthy rats have crossed the water by now. Let them go."

"But we were told to find everyone. You heard what our leader said. Kill the men and boys, and take the women and girls to our camp. That's what he said."

Nomi glanced at Mama, who was holding her three smallest children tightly against her chest. Her head was thrown back, her eyes closed, and her lips moving in silent prayer.

Take the women and girls to the rebel camp? Nomi turned this over in her mind. And then what? What would happen to them there? And no Baba or Andrau to protect them! They would be dead, all the big brothers and their strong baba. She swallowed at the hard lump forming in her throat.

Grandmother was praying, too. Nomi watched her mouth form silent words. Dorcas lay against a stone, maybe sleeping, maybe quaking in fear.

"I'm not going into that water," one of the rebels said. "Let's go back to the village."

There was no response, and in the silence – as the sun began to cast long shadows across the rocks – Nomi felt her muscles relax. Had the rebels gone? What a wonderful thing to be free of them!

But what would her family do now? Go back to the compound and rebuild the house and storage barns? Would they sit there and wait for another army of rebels to storm the village? Who could live in such constant terror?

"Nomi." It was Baba, whispering to her. He had stepped over a couple of his children and now squatted down beside her. "Is there another way out of this place?"

She blinked up at him, surprised to see the pain written across her father's beloved face. "I don't think so," she began, then halted. "Wait – I remember something. Do you see those two large stones over there? The ones near Dorcas? If you

45

move them, you'll find an opening. It leads to the stream and then to the forest on the other side. It's a very small space."

"Too small for Mama and Grandmother?"

Nomi tried to recall what she and Miriam had discovered one afternoon. They had been searching for boulders to use as writing desks for their pretend school. When Nomi pushed away the two stones, she had seen the opening.

"Yes, Baba," she told her father. "I think it's big enough for everyone. Even you."

"Little Lamb," he said, gently taking her hand. "Please forgive me for not listening to your plan. Your family has teased you a lot about your secret hiding places," Baba went on. "But now we're all benefiting from your cleverness. This is a very good one you found."

Nomi reflected on the hours she and Miriam had spent here – chatting, pretending to be in school, eating cookies and sucking on sugar lumps. How could such a wonderful place have been transformed into something so terrible – a secret den, a hole to escape from bad men who love to kill and burn?

Baba's touch on her arm drew her back to the present. "Nomi, you have saved your family."

"No, Baba, God saved us. It's like you said. We're under His wings."

Her father nodded. "Listen to me, now. Two of my sons and I are leaving this place. We have to look for Luke. We must find him – we will find him. Andrau will stay here with you." He signaled to his oldest son.

As Andrau began crawling toward them, Baba continued. "When we come back, we'll all go together to find another place to live. But Nomi, if you hear the soldiers again, you must push back the stones and leave this place. Don't wait for us. Go into the forest. Run, Nomi, run with your family. Try to find the next village. It's near the river. Maybe only half a day's walk upstream from where we are. You understand?"

Nomi nodded. This was a big responsibility for her. For one little goat-faced girl. "I will try."

"If we don't find you in the forest, we'll look in all the nearby villages. But don't continue to wait for us – not more than a single day. You must run again. Go to Uganda."

"Uganda?"

"It's another country – south of our homeland," Andrau cut in. He had joined her father. "Nomi, you and I, we'll ask everyone we meet where Uganda is."

"They have special camps there," Baba told her. "These camps are for families who have run from the rebels. You'll be protected. One day we will find you and join you there."

"But Baba, how can your family leave this hiding place without you?"

"I have no choice. It may take many days to find Luke.

47

More than anything, I want my family to be safe. In Uganda, we can begin a new life."

"But I don't want a new life," she said. "I want our old life."

Her father took her shoulders. "Little Lamb, we can't choose our future. It's in the hands of God. But you, my daughter, I want you to live. Live!"

He tightened his hands on her shoulders. Then before she could respond, he turned away and crept toward Mama.

❖❖❖

As night tiptoed across the hiding place, the littlest children began whimpering. They were hungry, they whined. They wanted to eat. They wanted to sit by a fire. They wanted to go home. A stern look from Mama silenced them.

The lump in Nomi's throat had turned to tears, and she was doing her best to wipe them from her cheeks. Now Baba and the other big brothers were gone. Everyone else in the family was safely tucked into this secret clearing among the stones. Everyone but Luke.

Where was her hot-headed brother? With all her heart, she prayed he was not harmed.

Dorcas's leg looked terrible. A bullet had gone right into the calf and come out the other side. Grandmother had bandaged the injured leg with a strip of fabric torn from her head scarf. Dorcas lay with her head on their mother's lap.

Nomi prayed she was sleeping. She thought about her last words to her sister.

"I hate you," she had shouted at Dorcas. "I hate you!" Now she knew how much she loved her sister. It was a deep passion, a love than only one sister can feel for another. More than anything, she wanted Dorcas to live a full, healthy life, with a good husband and many children of her own.

What if she died? People often died, even from small injuries. Infection was a terrible thing, and no one knew how to prevent it. Doctors and hospitals were many miles away. Much too far to walk.

Andrau elbowed Nomi. "I've made a decision. I'm going out to look for food."

Nomi gasped and caught his arm. "No, Andrau! You can't do that. You can't leave. Baba said you would keep us safe."

"Part of being safe is having food to feed those babies. If they don't eat soon, they'll cry even louder. I'm sure I saw some banana trees just near the river."

"Yes, they're not far. And there's a mango tree just at the edge of the forest. Andrau, please be quick!"

He nodded. After a whisper to Mama, he slipped over the rocks.

Hours passed . . . or what seemed like hours. Then Andrau's head appeared over the boulders. He jumped down into the clearing and began to hand out bananas, mangos, even some cookies.

Cookies? Nomi glanced up in surprise. "*Bisquets*, Andrau? Where did you . . . ? Did you go to our compound?"

He hunkered down beside her and handed over a banana. "I found these breads in our house. Mama bought them at the market last week, remember?"

"Our house is still there? They didn't burn it?"

"It's burned. But not all of it. The storage barns are mostly gone. The animals, too. They took them." He hung his head and chewed for a moment. "I found these *bisquets*, and nothing more."

"The beds?"

"Burned up."

"The cooking pots?"

"Gone."

"The goats? The sheep? What about the chickens?"

"No animals!" her brother barked. "I told you already."

Nomi found she couldn't eat her banana. Without their animals, her family had nothing. They traded their goats and chickens at the market for bread, oil, kerosene, sugar. Beans and corn were all very good, but animals? A man's wealth was in his livestock. Baba would be devastated.

"How can this be?" she asked her brother. Her voice quavered with anger. "How can someone be so wicked as to steal another man's animals?"

"Those men – they're the army of Satan, that's how. They kill, they steal, they burn. They will do anything it takes to drive us away from our homes." He nudged her. "Eat the banana. I risked my life for it, you know."

Nomi looked up to see a grin on his face. "That's not funny, brother. You did risk your life."

"Not much. It's quiet now. They've destroyed our village, and everyone is gone. Nothing's left. Why would they linger?"

"That's true." She brightened a bit. "And they would have no reason to return!"

"Oh, they'll come back. They know people. People love their homes, their land, their possessions. They know we'll return to our village if we think it's safe. That's when they'll attack again."

Nomi struggled with a question that had nagged her all afternoon. "Andrau, why do the soldiers take the women and girls to their camp? Why is that?"

Her big brother stopped chewing for a moment. "I don't know everything, Nomi," he murmured. "But I heard they sell them. They sell them for wives and servants. They make them into slaves. Men will pay good money for a new wife or a servant."

Nomi shuddered. "That's a wicked, wicked thing to do.

God will punish them."

In silence, she managed a few bites of her banana. Andrau had slumped back against a stone and seemed to be sleeping. Closing her eyes, Nomi leaned against her brother's arm. What would tomorrow bring?

CHAPTER SEVEN

Shouting broke through the thin mist of Nomi's sleep. She jolted awake.

"Where are they?" Someone yelled loudly, not far from her family's hiding place.

Fear stabbed through Nomi's heart.

"Just there, just there! In the rocks!"

Nomi barely had time to catch her breath before scrambling over her brothers and sisters toward the two boulders. Mama and Grandmother clamped their hands tightly over the babies' mouths.

"Look over at that place!" another man called out. "I think that's it!"

Andrau had clambered to Nomi's side and was helping her push away the boulders. The moment they had cleared the space, Nomi began feeding her brothers and sisters through it as fast as she could.

Someone shouted again. "No, not there! Up higher!"

Two of Nomi's older sisters shoved Dorcas's shoulders into the hole. Someone outside tugged her through the rest of the way. She was biting her lip to keep from screaming out in pain.

Grandmother followed Dorcas. Then Mama slipped through the hold.

"I've got it!" The man's voice crowed. "Yes, there they are!"

Ak-ak-ak-ak! Ak-ak-ak-ak! Ak-ak-ak-ak!

Gunfire erupted, bullets flying overhead. Andrau scooped Nomi up and pressed her through the hole. He followed as quickly as he could.

"They're getting away! You three – run around the rocks! Go to the other side!"

Nomi splashed through the shallow stream, grabbing stumbling babies and tossing them like grain sacks across to the other side.

"Go around! Around to the back!" the rebel leader cried.

Someone let out a whoop. "I see them! They're crossing the river! Everyone follow me!"

Andrau grabbed Nomi up in his strong arms and threw her head-first into the forest. She landed on a branch that broke beneath her. Before she could catch her breath, Andrau snatched her collar and slung her forward again.

Landing on her feet this time, she began to run. Blindly, she tore through the trees.

Ak-ak-ak-ak! Ak-ak-ak-ak! Ak-ak-ak-ak!

The awful sound was right behind her. Blam! A banana tree burst in half just as she passed it. She could see nothing. Only trees, trees, more trees.

"Nomi!" It was Andrau. He pushed her to the left. "That way! Run!"

"Where's Mama?"

"I don't know! Just run!"

Clenching her teeth, Nomi ran as fast as her bare feet could carry her. She could hear Andrau tearing through the brush beside her, but she couldn't see him. And suddenly the trees parted. Another stream lay ahead.

"Those rocks!" she cried out.

"No! Don't hide!" Andrau dragged her back into the forest.

They ran until Nomi's lungs felt as if they would burst open. Her legs were torn, bleeding. Her feet stumbled over stones and vines. She fell. She stood again.

She ran again. Faster, faster. Now she couldn't see Andrau! Where was he? Where was her family?

Ak-ak-ak-ak! Ak-ak-ak-ak! Ak-ak-ak-ak!

The gunfire was far away now. She could barely hear it. She stumbled and fell to her knees as she hurtled forward. Knowing she couldn't go on in this way, she threw herself up into a mango tree. Like a monkey, she climbed and climbed. Then she hung there, clutching the branches, breathing hard.

Where was her brother? Andrau had been with her only a short time ago. He was gone now. Far gone. She saw no one. Her whole family had vanished.

Swallowing back her fear, Nomi tried to think. Thirst

clutched at her throat. Spotting a ripe mango just down the branch on which she sat, she tugged it from its stem. She bit the tough green skin, tore the mango open, and gnawed on the sweet orange fruit.

Where was everyone? Mama? Grandmother? She looked around as she ate, scanning the shrubs for shapes of her loved ones. Surely they were near. But she could see nothing. Nothing but trees. Where were they?

Where was she?

The realization that she was lost hit Nomi hard. There were bad things in these forests. Bad snakes, for one – the red *bey-ar* that lifted its head before making the deadly strike, the black snake with two heads, the white snake with a black mouth. Dangerous animals lived here, too. Leopards and buffalo.

Staying in this tree was a bad idea, she knew, but where was she to go?

Working up her courage, Nomi called out. "Andrau! Where are you?"

No response.

"Mama? Grandmother?" She heard nothing. "Baba, are you near?"

For the first time since the attack, Nomi missed her little doll. Esther was gone, she realized, burned up. She would never see that yellow hair or those blue eyes again.

Everything was gone. All the places that were so important to her family and their village would have been burned to the ground. Her home. Her school. Her church.

How had God let this happen? Nomi felt angry and sad at the same time. She decided to pray. But as she bowed her head, she realized suddenly that Esther was not the only important possession she had lost.

Sunday afternoon on their way to church – before the rebels stormed the village – Grandmother had chosen Nomi to carry her precious Bible. With great care, Nomi held the book tightly against her chest. As the worship time began, she helped Grandmother peel back the layers of newspaper wrapped around it. They searched together for words Nomi could read. To her surprise, she had been able to sound out quite a few of them. Even better, she knew what they meant in her language.

"This word is *God*," she had whispered to Grandmother as she pointed out the strong G. "This one says, is. This one is *love*."

"That's a good thing," Grandmother told her. "God is love. That is well known."

God is good? If He was so good, Nomi thought as she sat in the mango tree, why did He let those rebels storm their village. Why was Dorcas shot? Why had He permitted Nomi to lose Grandmother's Bible? Though the family had escaped safely, the rebels had found Nomi's and Miriam's hiding place with no trouble. It was as if they knew exactly where to look.

That realization hit her straight in her stomach. The soldiers knew where to look. But no one knew about that place. No one but Nomi and Miriam. Had Miriam told them? Had she betrayed her best friend?

Nomi's eyes filled with tears. Miriam practiced the same religion as the rebel army. Her mother and father always gathered their family to pray at the correct hour, five times a day, and sent their sons to a special religious school on Saturdays. Miriam was faithful to her religion, even though she didn't understand its beliefs very well. Following her holy book's instructions, she wore her long-sleeved gowns and head scarves even on the hottest of days. After she gave Nomi the doll, she had refused to ever touch it again. It was *haram*, she said. Unclean. Instead, she made herself a baby out of a stone and wrapped it in old, ragged cloths.

Nomi brushed tears from her cheeks as she thought about the fun she and her best friend had enjoyed in their hideaway. Would Miriam have betrayed her? Had Miriam actually told the rebels where to find Nomi's family?

No, she would never do such a thing, Nomi decided. It was impossible that Miriam would have led killers straight to her best friend. Surely not.

❖ ❖ ❖

The sun hung overhead, its hot rays blazing through the canopy of trees. How far away would Nomi's family have gone? Surely they knew she was missing. But what if the soldiers had found them again?

There was really no choice. Nomi had to leave the tree and try to find a village. Only then might she learn where her family had gone. Despite their hard, tough soles, her bare feet felt the pain of the thorns, stones, and sharp grasses as she made her way through the forest.

Constantly, she looked around for snakes, but she could barely see ten feet in front of her through the dense undergrowth of the canopy. Were leopards watching her? Tracking her?

Nomi found a thick branch that had fallen from a tree, so she stripped it of leaves. It wasn't much of a weapon, she knew, but she felt a little braver carrying it. Occasionally she called out for her mama or baba. She yelled for Andrau even more loudly.

After many hours of walking, she realized the sun had begun to sink in the sky. Again she shouted, "Grandmother! Where are you?"

"I'm not your grandmother," someone called back. "But I'm here."

Nomi halted in surprise. It was a familiar voice, though she couldn't place it.

"Where are you?" she asked.

"Just near the big *lalop* tree."

"I see hundreds of *lalop* trees!" Nomi was so happy to hear what seemed like a friendly voice, that she couldn't help skipping as she made her way toward the sound.

Suddenly, she heard a whistle. Could that be her newfound companion? She whistled back.

Another whistle filtered toward her.

She formed her lips for a responding whistle, but at that moment, she spotted a form moving through the brush. Could it be . . .

"Peter?" she called. "Is that you?"

He stepped over a fallen tree trunk and gaped at her. "Nomi?"

"Yes, it's me." They stood in silence a moment. She noted the large machete tucked into his belt. That was a much better weapon than her stick.

"Peter, your face is covered with dried blood," she told him. "What happened to you?"

"They cut me just here." He pointed to a spot near the top of his forehead. "But I'm okay."

"Are you sure?" She stepped to his side, stood on tiptoe, and took a look at the gash. "It's not bleeding now. I think you'll be all right, Peter. Where is your family?"

"I don't know." He hung his head. "Some of them are

. . . they are dead. My mama. My smallest sisters. Our new baby. I saw what they did to them."

His shoulders hunched as he covered his face and began to cry. Nomi put her arm around him, but he pulled away and turned so she couldn't see his face. Despite her intention to comfort him, she started crying, too.

"I lost my family in the forest," she told him. "I think my best friend told the rebels where we were hiding near the river. They came after us this morning. We all ran together, but we got separated."

"I don't know where the rest of my family is, either." He swallowed back tears. "Where are you going, Nomi?"

"To a village."

"To our village?" He turned to face her. "It's just there, you know. Just beyond these trees."

"No, it can't be. I've been walking most of the day."

"Then you have been walking in a circle."

Nomi let out a breath. "Are you sure?"

"Yes, I crossed the river only a few minutes ago. After they cut me, I fell to the ground, and lay with the others. I pretended to be dead. I didn't move. The rebels left after they took the livestock and food and burned everything, but I waited all that night and most of the next day until I was sure they were not coming back. Then I found a shovel and buried my mother and my sisters."

"You did a good thing to bury them," Nomi told him. "But you must not remember them as they were at the end. They're happy now, because they're with Jesus."

"I know, but why —" He bit off his words. "Anyway, I searched the village until I found this machete and some food. I looked for anyone who might be alive, but there was no one."

"Did you see my brother, Luke, there? He didn't hide with us. Baba and Andrau left us near the river while they went to look for him. Did you see my baba or Andrau there among the people?" She blinked back a tear.

"They weren't there. So, don't worry. Maybe you'll see them soon." He studied her for a moment. "This is not the time to cry, Nomi. Let's go find the village where my auntie lives. I've been there before. I think I know the way."

CHAPTER EIGHT

But Peter did not know the way to his auntie's village. He and Nomi walked until the sun set. Then they climbed a tree and ate some more fruit. Both were so thirsty, their tongues so dry, they could hardly speak.

As night crept over the forest, they built a sturdy nest of strong branches knitted together and covered with leaves. It would not keep them safe from snakes and leopards, but it was better than lying on the ground.

❖❖❖

Nomi woke to the *plop* of a raindrop on her arm. Another splashed down near the first. And then, as if from a broken water gourd, rain poured from the sky. Nomi clambered down the tree and tore off a large banana leaf. She formed it into a cup. As the rain filled it, she drank and drank until her stomach hurt.

Peter had cut his own leaf and was doing the same thing. Then Nomi helped him wash the blood from his face with the fresh rainwater. She gently cleaned the gash on his head. It was a bad cut. She shook her head as she pondered what the soldiers had done to Peter. It was a miracle that he survived.

They began trudging through the rain toward the place Peter thought the village might be. The downpour tapered off eventually, and they began to look for something better than berries and *lalop* fruit to eat.

Stepping around a large bush, Nomi suddenly spotted

the distinct shape of a house. She caught her breath. There was another one!

"Peter!" She grabbed his arm and dragged him forward. "There it is! There's your auntie's village!"

He let out a whoop. "Come on, Nomi! Let's run!"

"Wait!" She caught the back of his shirt. "How do we know the rebels aren't there? We need to be careful how we approach."

"Of course," he said, letting out a breath. "You're right."

Crouching low in the tall green grass, they made their way toward the cluster of houses. The sounds of children laughing and cattle lowing, the clang of cook-pots and the smell of good food coming from the clearing near the *kornuk* let them know this village was still free from attack. As they pushed through the last of the grass, children began to gather around them.

"What happened to your head?" one boy asked.

"Is she your sister?"

"Why were you in the forest?"

Peter brushed aside their questions. "I'm looking for my Auntie Sarah."

"Sarah is just there," a girl said, pointing. "Is she your auntie?"

"Yes!" Peter set off in a trot, calling to her. Nomi

followed close at his heels.

Spotting her nephew, Auntie Sarah dropped her wooden paddle into the rice, trotted a few feet, and threw her arms around Peter. He pressed his head against her chest as she cooed and clucked over him.

When Peter was unable to speak, Nomi filled Auntie Sarah in on the events of the past days.

"Is anyone from our village here?" Nomi asked. "I'm looking for my mama and baba and the rest of our family."

Auntie Sarah's eyes softened. She was a large woman with soft skin and strong white teeth. She wore a faded pink dress with a blue shawl tied around it.

"My sweet child," she said to Nomi, "the only ones here from your village are you and Peter. I'm sorry to tell you this sad news, but maybe it will not be so bad. We'll pray for God to bring both of your families together again. And, you know, that is often what happens in the camps. These families who have been scattered find each other in the big camps. Sometimes, they're brought together when they register for resettlement."

"What is resettlement?" Peter asked.

Auntie Sarah shook her head as she peered at his head wound. "I want to put some medicine on that, my son. You must keep it covered from the flies."

"Resettlement, Auntie?" Nomi spoke up. "What is

that?"

"Let's not talk of such difficult subjects now, my children. You must have something to eat and drink. Follow me to the *kornuk*."

❖ ❖ ❖

Nomi ate until her stomach felt like a hard round soccer ball. Auntie Sarah had placed brown beans, green beans, yellow corn, and a mound of steaming *aseda* - a stiff white corn mush - on a mat before her and Peter. They dipped handfuls of *aseda* into a huge bowl of stew, laden with chunks of chicken and yams. When she put three fish each on the mat, Nomi almost couldn't eat them. But she did.

It was almost time for the children of the village to come into the *kornuk* to eat lunch, so Auntie spoke quickly. "You must not tell the other children what I say," she instructed. "They will be frightened."

Nomi nodded, beginning to be frightened herself. "What is it, Auntie?"

"The people of this village – most of the wives and children, some of the men and boys – we are all leaving here tomorrow. We will go together to the camp in Uganda. That's where we'll be safe, and there we will stay until we can return here, to our home."

"May we go with you, Auntie?" Peter asked.

"Of course you will. Along the way, we'll ask about

your families. There are many people on the roads these days, traveling to the camp. Maybe someone will have news."

"Auntie, what is resettlement?" Nomi asked.

The kind brown eyes turned to her. "Resettlement is when the governors of the camp send you to another country. You have to leave South Sudan. You must move out of Uganda, because that country's people want their land. They don't like refugees living in places where they could have farms and houses."

"What's a refugee?" Peter wondered.

"That is us. Refugees are those who can't stay in their village – or even in their own country – because there are too many bad people wanting to kill them."

"We used to be South Sudanese, but the rebels have turned us into refugees," Nomi stated.

"Yes, they have." Auntie scowled for a moment, but her lovely smile soon returned. "But God is with us, and He has a good plan for our future. So, we will go to the camp and stay there until He tells us His plan."

The children had come pouring into the *kornuk*, eager for their lunch and even more eager to talk to the two newcomers.

But Auntie Sarah would have none of it. "You come with me," she told Peter and Nomi as they finished their meal. "I'm going to put you in my house, and there you will sleep until

CHAPTER NINE

Though she was exhausted, Nomi couldn't sleep in the heat of the day. She lay awake listening to the sounds of the village – those familiar, much loved sounds of laughter and contented livestock and birds calling to one another. But this was not her village, her family, her friends, her cattle. Where was everyone now? Those that she loved, where had they all gone?

"I don't want to go to Uganda," Peter said in the low light of the thatched roof hut. "And I don't want to be resettled anywhere but our own village."

"I don't think we have a choice, Peter," Nomi said. "We can't go back."

"I will go back one day. If I have to stay in Uganda until I'm a man, I will take my wife and my children to that same village and there we will live until we die."

The thought of living in Uganda until she was grown startled Nomi. Is that what happened to refugees? Did they ever go home?

"Peter," she said, "Our village was destroyed by the rebels. It's gone. Almost everything is burned or stolen, and all the people who survived ran away."

"I don't care." Peter's voice was angry. "I will rebuild the whole village!"

"The forest will have crept through what's left and eaten it. You won't even be able to find it."

"Stop saying bad things, Nomi. I can find our village. I know I can."

She lay in the half-light, staring at a sunbeam filtering down from a small hole in the mud wall. "I hate Miriam," she said. "I hate her."

"Who?"

"Miriam, my best friend. Now my worst enemy. She told the rebels where to find my family."

"How do you know?"

"Because our hiding place was perfectly hidden. No one could have found it. But the rebels did. Miriam told them."

"Miriam – that trader girl?"

"Yes, her." Nomi squeezed her eyes shut, trying not to think about laughing, sweet Miriam. She would make herself forget the yellow-haired doll, the pretend school, the secret hiding place.

"I will never remember her again," she announced.

"And I'll never forget everything that happened to my family . . . to my mama." Peter let out a breath and fell silent.

Nomi fumed, remembering Miriam, despite her determination to forget. She would never have a best friend again. She would never trust anyone. In fact, she didn't even trust God now. Auntie Sarah had said good things about God's plans, but she had not heard bullets flying by her head or seen them bursting banana trees in half. She hadn't watched the smoke from her village as it burned to the ground. And she certainly hadn't lost her whole family.

Lying in silence, she heard Peter crying softly. He must have seen something terrible. Those rebels had killed his mother in a bad way. But how could anyone kill an innocent baby girl? Those men were demons. But God had let them loose in South Sudan, and He had stood by and watched them devour people and land and animals, and everything that made the world wonderful.

God, Nomi decided, was not good. He was not love, even though the Bible and Grandmother said He was. Auntie Sarah said God had good plans for His people. What kind of good plan was it to let a boy's mother and baby sister be murdered right in front of him? No, that kind of God could not be called good or loving.

As a knot of hurt and doubt settled down deep in her stomach, Nomi clenched her teeth. She would never trust anyone again, and she would never, ever pray to God.

❖ ❖ ❖

After a hearty evening meal, the oldest man of that village gathered Nomi, Peter, and the other children around him outside the *kornuk*. Their parents formed a half-circle behind them. Several of the other elders joined him as he took a seat on his special stool. Before him on a small table sat a Bible. At his side hung a large knife.

In a deep voice, the chief grandfather spoke. "Long ago, a beautiful weaver bird returned to his nest from a day of hunting for food. This bird had built his nest to hang from the branch of a large tree, and twenty-two other birds had built nests in the same tree. They all lived happily together, protecting their tree from snakes, and singing for joy when baby weaver birds hatched from their eggs.

"But on this one day when he returned to his nest, the weaver saw that his tree had been chopped down. Someone had turned it into firewood and taken it away, leaving only a few branches on the ground. The beautiful nests lay scattered here and there. All of them were destroyed. The birds who had lived in the tree had gathered around, mourning the loss of their tree and all their precious nests with eggs inside them."

The children, including Nomi and Peter let out a

collective groan. No one should ever cut down a weaver bird's tree. That was a very bad thing to do.

The old man continued. "The birds discussed their loss and one of them said he had seen a large tree some distance away. It was a perfect tree for weaver nests with long thin branches that would betray a snake at its first slither. After much talking, the birds made a decision. They flew far, far away from that fallen tree and made new nests in that bigger, better, and much safer tree."

Nomi knew the grandfather told this story to help the children when their families started for Uganda the next day. But she didn't believe she would ever find a better place to live than the house in her village.

"Tomorrow morning," the grandfather said, "we will begin a long journey to the south. We will go to Uganda. After we arrive there, we will build a new village. It will be a safe place away from the fighting that has overtaken South Sudan. Uganda is beautiful. It has rich soil and plenty of land. It will be our new home."

At that, he took the knife from its sheath and laid it on the ground. Everyone knew by this sign that the decision to leave the village had been made. Nothing could change it.

The children were unusually silent as they slipped away to their sleeping houses.

CHAPTER TEN

At dawn the next morning, Nomi jumped up from her pallet bed and ran to find Peter in the boys' sleeping house. She had hardly slept that night, and now she joined Auntie Sarah and the other families as they loaded their possessions on carts and hoisted heavy bundles onto their backs. Several goats and chickens had been chosen to make the journey, and as it turned out, one or two families were remaining in the village to look after the livestock that must be left behind.

The children around her were dancing with excitement over this big adventure. But Nomi could see the pain and sadness written in the eyes of their parents.

As the villagers set off down a dusty road, Nomi found Peter and matched his long pace. He wouldn't look at her.

"Do you know anything about Uganda, Peter?" she asked.

"Some."

"What do you know? Do they have villages? Are there big cities like Khartoum?"

"Some," he repeated.

"What are the names of the cities?"

"Kampala. That's the capital city. It's all I know."

"Is the refugee camp in Kampala?"

"Of course not."

Nomi frowned at his retort. "Well, why not?"

"No one wants refugees!" he said turning on her. "No one wants us. No one cares! The Uganda government will keep us away from cities where we could earn money or go to school or build nice houses. We will live inside a big fence in houses made of plastic."

"How do you know that?" Nomi tossed back. "Maybe there are strong stone houses in the camp. Maybe we'll have a big school with lots of teachers."

He laughed. "Sure. Maybe my baba and brothers will be waiting there for me, and I'll go to university and learn how to fly airplanes. I'll become the king of Uganda. Of all of Africa! How's that, Nomi? Do you think that will happen?"

She glared at him. "I don't know what will happen, but Auntie Sarah told us that God—" She caught herself, and stopped speaking. She was not going to think about God anymore, she remembered. "You're right, Peter. Life is going to be terrible."

Peter was carrying his auntie's cookpot and other kitchen items tied into a red patterned cloth. He shifted the load from one shoulder to the other. Nomi did the same with the roll of mats she was toting. They walked in silence for what seemed like hours.

Nomi could hear the other children laughing and calling out to each other. Occasionally some of them ran by, chasing each other, as the long trail of people moved quickly along the road. She wanted to comfort Peter, but she had no words for him. She wanted to believe God was good, but images of Dorcas's leg and Peter's wounded forehead flashed through her mind. She wanted to remember happy times, but when she tried, all she could think about was Miriam telling Abdul Big Nose where Nomi's family was hiding in the secret place near the river.

"And how are my two new children today?" Auntie Sarah's bright voice echoed behind.

Nomi looked over her shoulder to find Peter's auntie hurrying toward them with two big mangoes in her hands. "I'm glad to be traveling with your people, Auntie," she said. "This is a better journey than my last one - when I was lost in the forest."

"And what about you, Peter?" Auntie asked.

"I'm happy, too."

"Oh, you look happy, Peter. As happy as a leopard that just lost its antelope dinner to a pack of jackals."

He cracked a grin. "I'm happier than that, I think."

"Good. Then you will both enjoy these mangos for lunch. Maybe when we settle for the evening, we'll be able to cook some *aseda* and beans."

"How many days will we walk until we arrive in Uganda, Auntie?" Nomi asked.

"I don't know. No one from the village has ever been there. We only know the border crossing is in the south of our nation, and we think this is a good road to follow."

It occurred to Nomi that she was possibly just as lost now as when she was walking in circles in the forest.

"Peter is going to learn how to fly airplanes, Auntie," Nomi said. "From the sky, he'll be able to see all the roads to Uganda. Then no one will ever get lost."

"An airplane flier, Peter?" Auntie's voice held a note of laughter. "My goodness, you have a big future ahead."

"He's also going to be king of Uganda," Nomi added.

"King! Well, then I'm very happy to be your auntie. I'll live in your big house with you and fly in your airplane every day. Now, that is something to look forward to!"

Nomi giggled and even Peter gave a small chuckle. "And Nomi will be my servant," he added. "She'll wash cookpots in the river all day."

"No, I won't, because I'm going to be a teacher." As the words spilled from her mouth, Nomi realized how nice they sounded. That was a good idea.

"In fact, I'm already a teacher," she continued. "I taught the alphabet and numbers and even some English to my best fr—"

"Who?" Auntie asked. "I'm sorry. I didn't hear you."

"We were just playing," Nomi said. "It was only a pretend school."

"That's a good place to start. Everyone knows that when children play, they practice what they will do when they become big. You will be a very fine teacher, Nomi."

"When you were young, did you want to do anything special, Auntie?"

"I did. I wanted to be a wife and a mama. I wanted many cows and a nice house. And you see, I have all those things!"

But even as Auntie spoke the bright words, Nomi knew that all three travelers had realized at once that Auntie Sarah had now lost almost everything. Her childhood dreams had been left behind in a village that was almost certainly doomed.

"In Uganda, you will have a nice new house," Nomi said, trying to sound encouraging.

"And you still have all your family," Peter added.

At that moment, a loud boom echoed through the air. Then another, followed by that familiar sound - ak-ak-ak-ak!

Someone shouted, "Rebels! Run! Run into the forest!"

The crowd along the road erupted into screaming and shouting. Babies began to wail. Nomi heard chickens squawking as Peter grabbed her hand and pulled her into the forest. Gunfire popped all around them. A mortar shell exploded so close the spray of mud and branches hit them in the face. They must hide - and quickly!

Nomi had not run more than a hundred feet when she spotted it. A fallen tree lay on the ground, its huge trunk almost hidden by brush.

"Peter!" she hissed. "Come!"

Now it was her turn to drag him toward the decaying log.

"No, it's too dangerous!" he said. "They'll find us!"

"They'll find us if we don't!"

She refused to let herself think of what might be lurking inside the rotten hollow trunk of the tree. Instead, she dived headfirst into it, grasping for handholds as she squiggled through the dark, musty space. Peter had followed her in, and she knew she must make room for him. She had to go as deep as she possibly could.

As she wedged herself tightly into the trunk, she heard men's voices. They called to each other as they pushed through the trees in search of livestock and people. Nomi squeezed her eyes shut. She knew if they found Peter, he would be killed or taken immediately to become an unwilling soldier in their rebel camp. She could not let herself think about what might happen to her.

And then she felt it. The sting of biting ants. Though she could see nothing, she knew they were crawling over her arm and up the sleeve of her shirt, biting her as they traveled. The pain grew intense as more and more of them sank their jaws into her tender skin. She wanted to scream, but if she did, the soldiers would find her. They would take Peter. The ants swarmed her now, biting her neck and shoulders as they marched down her back.

She bit her lip and began to cry in silence as the pain flooded her body. But outside, she could hear two men talking. They had paused, lit cigarettes. The smoke smell drifted into the log. They seemed to be standing near it.

"Dear God," Nomi prayed in desperation. "Please, please help me. I'm dying inside this tree. The ants are eating me. Please make the men move! Please send them away."

But even as she prayed, she felt the log tilt a bit. Even more agitated by the movement, the ants began to cover Nomi's legs. The wood suddenly splintered just above her head. The men were sitting on the log!

Nomi felt sure she would fall unconscious from the

agonizing, searing pain. Her whole body was on fire. She couldn't breathe. She couldn't move her head. Ants began to fill her mouth, her nostrils.

"Ow!" One of the men cried out. "Ow, ow! Biting ants. They're stinging me!"

The men jumped up from the log, rolling it slightly. Then their voices faded as they ran into the forest. The moment they were out of earshot, someone grabbed Nomi's foot. Peter, she prayed. Her head swam as he dragged her out of the log. She lay limp on the forest floor as he jumped and smacked at the ants on his own face, but he quickly knelt to Nomi's side, brushing and brushing as the insects swarmed over her.

In a moment, he lifted her up into his arms and threw her over his shoulder. "Come on, Little Lamb," he murmured. "Please don't die."

Nomi's world went black.

CHAPTER ELEVEN

The smell of meat cooking filled her nostrils. Nomi tried to focus, but it was dark and her eyelids were so swollen she let them close again. She had seen only that her whole body was covered in sticky black mud, and it felt wonderful. Cool water lapped near her face.

Voices drifted. "I think she's awake now," someone said.

"Let her sleep. Don't touch her."

"She'll be hungry." That was Peter speaking. "I know Nomi very well. She likes to eat."

Someone lifted her shoulders, shoving something soft under them so she was tilted up a little. "Open your mouth, Little Lamb," Peter said in a low voice.

She tried to see him as she obeyed. He pushed a small chunk of meat into her mouth. Antelope, she thought, chewing as best she could.

With every bite, awareness grew, and she began to remember what had happened. The rebels, the shooting, the fallen log, the ants. But where was she now? Who were these people she couldn't see?

"Let me feed her." It was Auntie Sarah's gentle voice. "I've had more practice caring for sick ones."

Auntie was with them! Nomi heart flooded with joy. She opened her mouth as Peter's sweet aunt fed her bit by bit. As she lifted her head to swallow water from a cupped leaf, Nomi felt a droplet fall on her cheek. Then another. But this wasn't rain. Auntie was crying.

"Oh, no," Nomi thought. The rebels had succeeded again. The people of Auntie's village had been scattered. Some, no doubt, were dead. She reached up and touched Auntie's face.

"God sent the ants to bite the soldiers," she murmured, suddenly confident in the One she had tried to abandon. "They ran away. God *is* watching us, Auntie, even if we don't always feel Him nearby."

The older woman nodded. "Yes," she said. "We are under His wings. But sometimes . . . oh, sometimes the jackals come."

❖❖❖

The next morning, Nomi opened her eyes to find a

small group of people around her, talking in low tones, moving back and forth from a nearby stream.

"You must wash yourself." Peter crouched at her side. His dark eyes were troubled. "Wash away the old mud. Put on some new, and as it dries we'll walk together. You can walk, can't you?"

"I'll do my best," she said, forcing herself up to her knees and then to her feet. "Are we still going to try to go to Uganda?"

"We have nowhere else to go," he said. "We can't find most of the people from Auntie's village, but some are surely alive. Her children are with us, and her husband is here, too, Uncle Simon. She hasn't found her mother and father."

Pondering the sorrow and fear everyone felt, Nomi crouched by the stream and washed as well as she could. Her eyes were still slits and the swollen ant bites in her nose made it hard to breathe well. After her simple bath, she spread mud over her skin again. Her church uniform was tattered and stained. The skirt hung from her waist, its hem torn so that it sagged almost to her ankles on one side.

The silent group collected what few belongings they still had and set off to find the road. Such an open space was dangerous, the men decided, so they all crept forward in the forest alongside the road. At night, they went farther into the trees, searching for berries and other fruit. They slept in a huddle, but Nomi never felt safe.

Many days passed as they pushed through the forest, always keeping the road in sight a short distance away. During the heat of the day, the sun beat down on them and a misty steam rose from the thick undergrowth.

One late afternoon, they spotted a group of five people making their way through the forest on the other side of the road. Everyone halted, frozen in fear. But after many minutes of careful study, Auntie let out a cry of joy. These were people from their village! At that, the other group began to shout their names and dance toward them across the road.

Nomi held her breath as they came near, clearly visible in the open space. Loud singing erupted as the two groups united. Even Peter had to smile at the great gift God had given in bringing their village back together. Of course, many were still missing, and the men shared information about what had happened after the attack. Then they sorted through several plans, deciding finally that they would continue along the road, hoping they were headed toward Uganda.

❖❖❖

"Stop, Peter!" Nomi whispered. "What is that?"

They had been walking for so many days she had lost count. Now and then, a truck or car sped along the road, but the group always kept to the forest.

"I don't see anything," Peter said.

"Look! Just beyond the tallest *lalop* tree. Houses - big ones. Three I think."

At that moment, the men halted the group. In low voices, they discussed this situation. Finally, Uncle Simon told the others, "The women, children, and men will stay hidden. I will go and see if someone is there."

At that, Auntie Sarah gave a little squeak. But everyone knew there was no use in arguing. When the men made a decision, it must be obeyed.

The group crept as close as they dared. Then Uncle Simon stole ahead of them through the forest until the cover of trees ended. Nomi found a place where she could watch him walk across the open space. As he neared the settlement, a man stepped around from behind one of the houses. He had a gun!

Nomi held her breath. Flashes of the past made her suddenly dizzy - running through the forest, losing sight of her family, the sound of gunfire . . . No! Stop! Squeezing her eyes tightly shut, Nomi let out her breath and forced herself to think about what was happening now.

The man with the gun had not fired. Instead, he and Uncle Simon were speaking calmly. Uncle Simon nodded and pointed in the direction of the forest. Finally, he returned to the group.

"We are in Uganda," he announced.

Everyone gasped at the same time. How could it be

that they'd left South Sudan and passed into Uganda without even knowing it? Was there no fence? No border guard? Did this mean they were safe now? Completely safe? Nomi's eyes filled with tears of thankfulness that God had done this miracle for this small, frightened group of villagers.

"I spoke to the watchman of that compound," Uncle Simon continued. "He is that man with the gun. He told me the owner is very rich. He owns five houses and many cows. Nearly one hundred."

At that, everyone gasped again. What a lot of cows! Nomi realized he was surely the wealthiest man in all of Uganda. How wonderful that God had brought them to this house! This very house!

Uncle Simon nodded. "The rich man's name is Wilson. Mr. Wilson. He's the grandson of a man who came to Uganda many years ago. The guard told me we aren't far from the refugee reception center. It's the place refugees must go before they're permitted to enter the camp. His employer owns a large truck, and he will probably send one of his men to drive us to the reception center. Mr. Wilson has done this before. Many South Sudanese go to his house, and he helps them. He is a man of God."

As these words of hope and joy filtered into everyone's minds, Auntie Sarah began to sing. The other women joined in, and the men began to dance. Soon everyone was dancing down the road, singing and whooping with happiness.

Nomi sang as loudly as anyone else. As her tired feet skipped along the hard path, she realized why she was so happy. It was because now, finally, the small flicker of hope in her heart had burst into flame. If she really did make it all the way to the refugee camp, maybe - just maybe - she would find someone she knew. Her mama and sisters, perhaps. Maybe her baba. At the thought of his kind face and gentle hands, tears spilled from Nomi's eyes. And she let herself cry and cry until finally Peter came to her side and put his arm around her shoulders.

"Nomi," he said, "you and I will stay together. When we get to the camp, we'll search for your family and mine. And maybe we'll find them."

❖❖❖

By the time the tired group had gathered inside a large room in the biggest of the houses, the sun had almost set. They stood huddled in a corner, the men in front, in case this wonderful event turned out to be a trick.

Nomi couldn't help but stare. The walls of the room were painted green. No mud to be seen here. Chairs covered in beautiful red fabric surrounded a low table made of some kind of dark wood she had never seen. Every window gleamed with shining glass, something she had only seen in the town where her mama went to shop.

As Nomi was admiring the long lengths of curtain fabric hanging beside each window, the door suddenly opened. Into the room walked a man unlike any she had ever seen in her life. His skin was totally white.

"Good evening," he said, speaking Arabic very badly. He wore a brown shirt and brown trousers, and he had thick leather shoes on his feet. He folded his arms across his large stomach. Beside him stood a small white lady with heaps of white hair like clouds on her head.

"So, you've come from South Sudan?" the man asked.

Uncle Simon stepped forward. "Yes, sir, Mr. Wilson. We're looking for the refugee camp in Uganda."

"It's not far. You'll like it there, I think." The man continued to speak in Arabic, but his words were difficult to understand. "The Ugandan government is working hard to provide homes and land for refugees - until you're able to safely go back to your country, of course."

"Yes," Uncle Simon said.

As the men talked, Nomi realized how much this rich man looked like her doll. He had the same yellow hair and blue eyes. His skin was so pale that he looked almost like a dead man.

"In the morning, I'll send you along to the reception center in one of my trucks." The man stroked the straight yellow hairs of his mustache. "After that, you'll go to the refugee camp. You can stay the night in the workers' compound. I don't have beds for you, but . . . well, you don't look as if you've slept in a bed for a long time."

Mr. Wilson's little wife looked at all of them with her own pair of blue eyes. She shook her head sadly and gave a little click of her tongue. "You've had a rough time of it - I can see that. We're so sorry for you. This should be a new beginning. The start of a better life."

"Yes, we do hope so," Mr. Wilson agreed. "Well then, good evening."

Without further words, the two left the room, shutting the door behind them. Nomi couldn't imagine a better life than the one she had known in her own village with her beloved family surrounding her. But Mr. Wilson's wife was right about one thing. This would be a new beginning.

CHAPTER TWELVE

The reception center turned out to be a very busy place. A large sign rose from the ground outside a wire fence, and Nomi tried to read it. The letters at the start of each word were U, N, H, C, and R. The words were too long and written in English, so she finally gave up and asked someone what it said. *United Nations High Commissioner for Refugees*, she was told. The one who read the sign told her that the UNHCR was the organization that helps refugees. Nomi decided these were words worth remembering, so she took a small stick and scratched them onto the dry skin of her arm where they would stay until the next time she washed it.

As she practiced reading and saying aloud the words, Nomi studied all the African and pale-skinned people wearing UNHCR badges on their shirts. They hurried about with notebooks in their hands and lines of worry between their eyebrows. Many, many South Sudanese people - more than Nomi had ever seen in one place - stood in long lines that led into white tents with blue plastic roofs. She felt sure that all the refugees from South Sudan must be at this place. And that meant her family might be here, too.

Nomi searched the long lines for anyone she recognized, but no one from her own village was to be seen. As she studied the rows of people, she realized that many were not from South Sudan after all. When asked, some stated their homeland as Central African Republic or Congo or Ethiopia. Others were dressed in Muslim clothes, and Nomi realized they might be from northern or western Sudan or Somalia.

The band of travelers from Auntie Sarah's village lined up and waited long, hot hours until finally they were led into the tent. As an official wearing a UNHCR nametag greeted the men, Auntie Sarah bent down and whispered to Nomi and Peter.

"I will tell the people at the reception center that you two are my own children," she said. "It is the custom of our people, you know, for relatives to welcome children like you into our family."

Nomi knew this was true, and part of her was happy to be adopted in this way. But she hoped to find her own mama one day.

A tired-looking young South Sudanese woman wearing

one of the UNHCR badges told Auntie Sarah that the children's true family names and information must be collected. That way, if Nomi's or Peter's family members were looking for them, they might be able to find them. And UNHCR could possibly help.

"We will keep your names in our files," she told Nomi and Peter, "and our computer will try to match you with your parents. Your names will also be entered onto a resettlement list. Maybe in a few years we'll put you on an airplane and send you to America. Or Australia. Or maybe Canada. You'll have a new life there, with many good things like schools and hospitals and jobs."

Nomi had heard of only one of the places mentioned: America. The thought of living by herself in a strange place where everyone spoke in English frightened her almost more than the thought of rebel soldiers. As the group was ushered outside the tent, Peter stepped to her side and took her hand. He shook it hard, as if making a pact with her, and didn't let go.

"Wherever we travel, Nomi," he told her, "you and I will go together. If we can't find our families, we will become a family. The two of us. I won't go to Canada and let them send you to America. We'll go to the same place."

At Peter's wise words, Nomi's heart softened and her discomfort melted a little. "Agreed," she said, giving Peter's hand a firm shake of her own. "We are a family, you and me. If we leave Uganda and fly to America on an airplane, together we'll search for food in the rivers and forests of that land. You can hunt birds or antelopes, and I'll make the fires to cook them. That way we'll have enough to eat. We'll make a catchment to hold rainwater so we can save it for drinking."

"We can build a compound with storage huts and a house for ourselves, too." Peter squared his shoulders. "Even though I'm a boy, I know how to cut the wood and put on the mud to make walls. It takes two to build a house."

Nomi liked this idea. "It won't be hard if we work together. I'm sure there will be dirt and water in America. We can make our own mud. If they have no cows in that country, we will mix the dung of elephants or buffalos into the mud to make the house strong."

Peter nodded. "In a year or two, when you're old enough, Nomi, I will marry you. Then we and our children can build ourselves a whole new village. We'll make a *kornuk* and a school and a church."

"That sounds like a good plan," Nomi agreed, even though the thought of marrying Peter or anyone else made her stomach tighten. But she knew people got married to have children, and Nomi did like the idea of holding her own babies in her arms. "I think you'll make a good husband."

"If we're living in America, you won't have any other

choices." He gave a shrug and grinned.

At that, Nomi giggled. What a strange conversation to have. It was her first discussion in Uganda, and she had agreed to marry Peter. Life had become so odd that she began to believe almost anything could happen.

It was at that very moment, Nomi caught sight of something that made her heart stumble. A tall man. A man she knew. She squinted her eyes against the bright sun and stared at the long line of people in the distance. No, it couldn't be. It wasn't possible.

She took a few steps forward, and suddenly the man moved. He turned his head toward her. He bent and spoke to someone beside him.

"Oh, Peter!" she gasped out. "Look who's there."

"Who?" He squinted in the direction she was pointing. "Who is it?"

"It's Abdul Big Nose!"

"Who? Where?"

"Abdul Big Nose is standing there in that line. He's wearing a blue robe. Do you see him?"

"I see a man with a very big nose, but I don't know who he is."

"He's one of those traders from the north. The ones who come down to sell at the big market."

Now her heart was hammering inside her chest. "And

that . . . that little person beside him . . . that's her. That's Miriam!"

As Nomi spoke the name, the one in a long robe and headscarf turned toward her. Yes, it was Miriam. No doubt about it.

Nomi swallowed hard. That was the very same Miriam who had been her best friend . . . Miriam who had betrayed Nomi's hiding place and put her family into the hands of the rebel soldiers.

"I don't know either one of them," Peter said. "But I think that lady down the row sold sweets. And that man behind her used to trade my mother kerosene for cassava flour."

They both fell silent. Nomi noticed that Miriam was staring at her intently now. She shielded her eyes with her hand as she studied the two in the distance. Then her face broke into a wide smile, and she gave a little wave.

"Nomi!" she called. "Hello, Nomi!"

Nomi stiffened and clenched her teeth. Without a word, she turned her back on her old friend and began walking toward Auntie Sarah. Peter caught her arm.

"Nomi?"

"What, Peter?" She jerked her arm away. "Do you want to know why I don't greet Miriam? Why I'll never speak to her again? It's because she told the rebel soldiers where my family was hidden after the attack."

"Really? Are you sure?"

"Of course I'm sure. We were inside the best hiding place in all of South Sudan. No one could have found us there - no one but Miriam. She betrayed me, Peter. Because of her, my family became separated from each other, and I lost them all. All! Miriam destroyed my family, Peter!"

"But you don't know that for sure. Maybe the rebels just found your hiding place."

"No. That's not possible." She shook her head. "Miriam told, and for that, I hate her. I hate, hate, hate her. I always will."

"What's this?" Auntie Sarah cut into the conversation and handed Nomi a roll of mats. "Take this, girl, and stop all that talk of hating. Be thankful for what God gave you - this friend from your village, me and my family, a safe journey to Uganda, and now a new home of our own. Here, Peter, take these blankets."

She pushed a heavy load of gray blankets at him and turned back into the huge crowd that had surrounded a truck marked on the side, UNHCR. Four men stood inside the truck bed and handed out mats, blankets, cookpots, bags of food, farming tools, and rolls of plastic. Uncle Simon and the other men had forced their way near the front of the pushing, shouting crowd. When they received supplies, they handed the items from one man to another until Auntie Sarah and her friends took them for safekeeping.

Nomi hugged her mats and tried not to think about Miriam. Of all the people she had prayed to find in Uganda, Miriam was the very last. No, Miriam wasn't even on the list. A knot of anger and hurt grew in Nomi's throat, and she swallowed back the tears that threatened.

How could Miriam have come to Uganda? Why would those traders travel here as refugees? They were surely safe enough - with all their guns and big trucks and loads of things to sell. Who would want to kill them?

They couldn't be war refugees like Nomi. Impossible. They weren't even from South Sudan. Nobody was trying to kill them. Were they?

As she stood turning over these thoughts, Nomi felt a tap on her shoulder. She swung around, the roll of mats thumping Miriam right in the stomach.

"Oof!" she cried out. Then she laughed, her warm brown eyes twinkling. "Are you trying to knock me down, Nomi?"

Without giving her old friend a moment to speak, Miriam continued. "I was hoping to find you, Nomi! I knew you had been forced out of your village. We passed through it on our way here, and we saw that everyone . . . everyone who escaped . . . had gone into the forest. When my father heard what had happened to your people, how those evil men attacked them and burned everything, he decided we also should go to Uganda."

"But why?" Peter asked, when Miriam took a breath. "Why would you leave South Sudan?"

"When we're in our own part of South Sudan –Darfur - we know the people living not far away hate us. My mama told me that a few years ago, the Sudanese government ordered my people to fight your people. We were supposed to kill you and take your land, but we refused. We said, no, they are our brothers. So the government sent the army to attack us. Many got killed or ran away, and we still aren't safe. Even though that war ended, our government doesn't like us, and Mama's afraid all the time. That's why Baba decided it was time for a new beginning."

Miriam finished speaking and let out a breath. "I'm so glad you're here, Nomi. Look what I have for you! I brought it all the way from your village."

She drew a small packet wrapped in newspapers from inside her robes. With a laugh of joy, she held it out for Nomi. "Open it!"

Nomi set the roll of mats on the ground and took the packet. She didn't know what to say or even what to think. Was Miriam her enemy or her friend?

As she peeled back the newspapers, Nomi sucked in a breath. "Esther!"

Miriam laughed. "I found her in your bean storage hut. It hadn't burned, and I'm sorry to say this, but we decided to take everything from the village that we could find for our journey. When the men opened the bean hut, Esther came tumbling out. So I grabbed her and hid her. And now, I give her to you again!"

Nomi stared down at the doll, unable to believe her eyes. Nothing made sense. Miriam had told the rebels about the hiding place - but here she was in Uganda, a refugee, too. The village had burned - but here was Esther. How could this be?

"We found something else that belongs to you, Nomi," Miriam said. "Can you come with me?"

Though Nomi had been unaware of it, Peter was standing just behind her. Now he took the mats and urged her to go with Miriam. He would make sure Auntie Sarah's family wouldn't leave her behind.

CHAPTER THIRTEEN

"Nomi, why aren't you talking to me?" Miriam asked as they crossed to another truck, this one filled with men passing out supplies to Miriam's people. "Are you sad about leaving your village?"

"I'm sad about losing my family," Nomi managed.

"They're not here? Near that truck where I found you?"

"No. I traveled with those people, but they're not my family."

Miriam took Nomi's hand and led her to the shade beneath a large tree. "Then I think you'll be happy with what we brought you from your village."

Miriam pointed to a mat on which lay a woman who was curled up in a ball, her face covered by a scarf. Nomi knelt to the side of the mat and lifted the fabric.

"Grandmother!" she cried out. Unable to hold in her joy, she threw her arms around the old woman. "Oh, Grandmother, it's me, Nomi! We're together again! You're here in Uganda and so am I!"

Grandmother opened her eyes a little, and a soft smile played across her mouth. "Little Nomi? Is it really you?"

"Yes, Grandmother!" At the look in Grandmother's soft eyes, Nomi buried her face in the old woman's neck and wept until she thought she could never cry again. "Oh, Grandmother, you're alive. You're here! But why are you lying down? Are you hurt? Can you come with me now? In the forest, I found Peter from our village, and some of his family is with him. We can join them. We'll build a house, and you can live with us until we find Baba and Mama and everyone else."

Grandmother's eyelids drifted shut. "I would like that very much, Nomi. But I'm sick now. There's a hospital at the refugee camp, and that's where I'll live until I'm better."

"Then I'll stay in the hospital with you."

"That would make me happy, but the doctors won't let you stay. There are too many sick people in the hospital. You go with your friend's family. Help them. When I'm better, you and I will live together."

"Then I'll visit you every day," Nomi said. As she spoke, she noticed a bundle wrapped in cloths lying under her grandmother's arm. "What is this?"

"Open it. You'll see."

Nomi pulled the fabric apart. In her lap lay Grandmother's Bible—the very one she had been carrying when the rebels attacked. But how could it be here? She had dropped it and never expected to see it again.

"After we ran into the forest," Grandmother said, "I lost everyone. So I returned to the village. I walked around to see if I knew any of the people who . . . who had not been able to get away. That's when I saw my Bible waiting there on the muddy path for me. I picked it up, and just then these good people came to the village in their trucks." She gestured toward Miriam and her family.

"Good people?" Nomi asked.

"Oh, yes, they're very good. They brought me all the way to Uganda. They gave me medicine and food. They washed my face when I had fever. They're my friends now. My family. Miriam helped me clean and wrap my Bible. She told me about you, and we realized that her Nomi and mine were the same. And now we're all together. God is good!"

"Baba says it's time to go," Miriam announced. She had left them alone for a few minutes, but now she reappeared with her usual grin. "Nomi, you and your grandmother will go with us to the camp. Then we'll put Grandmother into the hospital, and you can join Peter's family."

"That will be all right," Nomi agreed reluctantly. She was so used to hating Miriam that she hardly knew what to think of this cheerful, kind person who was acting just like the best friend she had always loved.

"Oh, don't look so sad," Miriam comforted her. "We'll see each other at the school. Yes, I'm going to school! Baba said so!"

She jumped up and down a few times and clapped her hands. Nomi couldn't help but laugh.

"You won't have to teach me how to speak English anymore," Miriam crowed, "because I'll be learning in a real classroom with a real teacher. Won't it be wonderful? We can sit together during our lessons and play outside when school is finished for the day. It will be just like always!"

Nomi shook her head. "I'm happy for you, Miriam," she said. And she was.

❖ ❖ ❖

Nomi's first days in the UNHCR refugee camp saw her busy from dawn to sunset. After settling Grandmother in the long, concrete block hospital where too many people slept side by side on cots or mats, Nomi rejoined Auntie Sarah's family.

The government of Uganda gave each family a small plot of land to call their own. Nomi worked alongside Peter and the others to build a house of mud and grass. Then they all dug up the soil of their new farm.

The sun burned down on Nomi as she collected stones that appeared beneath the hoes and shovels turning over the earth. As she piled up the stones, she listened to the songs filling the air around the new house. Songs about God's kindness. God's faithfulness. God's forgiveness.

At night, Nomi tried to sleep, but she was tormented by dreams of running through trees and jumping over streams as dark shadows chased her until she woke up screaming. Drenched in sweat, she lay awake praying that God would heal Grandmother and help Nomi find her family.

"What's wrong with you?" Peter asked her one day as she knelt stacking stones into a pile. "Auntie Sarah says you don't sleep, and you're not eating enough. She thinks you're sick."

"I'm not," Nomi said, lifting a particularly heavy rock onto the stack. "I can't help what I dream."

Peter settled onto the ground beside her and let out a sigh. "I have bad dreams, too. And when I'm clearing brush or digging, I see those men killing my mother and my sisters. I see it every day, over and over."

"You're always singing, though."

"I'm trying to keep my thoughts on better things."

Nomi studied him. Though the wound on his head had healed, she knew Peter would always carry the wound of the terrible things he had seen. That injury could never heal completely. They were children of war.

"After church tomorrow," Nomi said, "I'm going to the hospital to see my grandmother. Will you come with me?"

Peter nodded. "Thank you, Nomi."

"We start school next week. I've been wearing these same clothes for many weeks. This was my Sunday School uniform."

One side of Peter's mouth tipped up as he studied the gray rags she wore. There was almost no color left, the hem of her skirt had torn all the way around, and a tattered strip that might have been her collar hung down her back.

"It used to look better," he said.

"Yesterday Auntie Sarah gave me a new school uniform from the UNHCR. She said I could wear it to church since I don't have anything else nice."

"I have new blue pants, too. And a yellow shirt."

Now it was Nomi's turn to smile at his missing sleeve and the large holes at the knees of his current trousers.

"You'll see Miriam at school," Peter said. "Have you forgiven her?"

"I don't even know if she told those men about our hiding place."

"Does it matter? We have to forgive people no matter what. That's what Uncle Simon told me. He said I have to forgive the men who killed Mama or I will allow them to continue harming my family. But this time the one they will be killing is me. God commands us to forgive, he said, not for the people who hurt us but for ourselves."

"I don't understand that," Nomi said.

"I had to think about it a lot."

"Did you forgive them?"

"Not yet, but I'm trying. If I don't forgive, what they did will stay in my brain and slowly eat me up. Like those ants ate you."

Nomi shuddered. "How do you do it?"

"When a bad thought comes about those men, I say to them, 'You killed my Mama and my baby sisters, but you won't kill all of us. You won't kill me. I won't hold onto what you did and hate you forever. I will let it go, so I can be free from every thought of you. God will help me do this.' That's what I say. And I say it all day long."

"I'll say it, too, Peter. It will be my prayer."

"You could say it to Miriam."

Nomi shrugged. "Maybe."

"I'll meet you after church tomorrow." Peter stood. "We'll go see Grandmother."

❖ ❖ ❖

Wearing her bright yellow dress with a blue stripe down the front, Nomi walked out of the cool shade of the church and into the hot sun. She stood for a moment, trying to find Peter. Instead, she saw someone in a purple scarf and robe hurrying toward her.

"Miriam?"

"There you are!" Miriam caught her hands. "I couldn't find your house, and we are working ourselves to death building our house and planting maize. Oh, trading is so much easier than farming!"

She laughed and shook her head before continuing. "I knew you'd be at church today, so I've been waiting for you. I have to tell you my good news!"

"What is it?" Nomi squeezed her friend's hands.

"Baba says I don't have to marry Abdul! At least not until I'm finished with my schooling. Can you believe it? That man was pushing my father to let him marry me next month! He said I should marry young so I can have as many babies as possible. I told him I wanted to go to school first, and then I would have babies. So Abdul got angry and hit me! See?"

Nomi gasped at the dark mark Miriam pointed out. It was on her cheek, carefully covered by her scarf. "Oh, Miriam! That's terrible." Before she could think, Nomi threw her arms around her friend and hugged her tightly. "I'm so sorry!"

"But it turned out to be a good thing, because I showed this mark to Baba just before Abdul came to see him. My father was so angry that he told Abdul I would go to school for as many years as I wanted to, and if he ever harmed me again,

Baba would not allow him to marry me."

"That's wonderful!" Nomi hugged her again. "Maybe you'll be a teacher one day."

"Yes, or a shopkeeper with a house of my own."

Nomi laughed at such a crazy idea. "What about a car?"

"Of course! I'll have my own car and drive everywhere I want to go. That will teach Abdul not to hit me!"

She and Nomi skipped around in a circle, just as they always had when they were happy. But they had only taken half a turn when Nomi stopped, bowed her head, and covered her face with her hands.

"Nomi?" Miriam said. "Are you all right?"

"I forgive you, Miriam. I know what you did, and I don't know why, but I want to still be your friend. So, I forgive you."

In the silence following her outburst, Nomi lifted her head. Miriam looked stricken.

"What?" she whispered. "What did you say?"

"You told the rebels about our hiding place. I know you did. But I want to forgive you, and I will. I want to be your best friend again, just like we were before."

At that, Miriam covered her face with her shawl and sank down onto the ground. Nomi fell to her knees beside her.

"It's true," Miriam sobbed. "Those evil men found us in town. They made us stand in a row facing them. They said they would kill all of us if we didn't tell where your people were hiding. No one said anything, because no one knew where any of you had gone, and they shot three of us just like that. The woman who sold sugarcane, remember? They killed her and her husband and their baby. And they walked down the row pointing their guns in our faces and shouting at us. And they said they would kill us if no one talked, and no one did, and that's when I told them about our hiding place."

Miriam was crying so hard her shoulders shook. Nomi stared at her friend. So, it was true. It was really true. Miriam had betrayed her family. Her best friend had sent those rebel soldiers straight to the place where they were hiding.

Nomi looked up into the sky. The blue, blue African sky. She saw a hawk soaring overhead, writing circles in the air. God lived up there somewhere, and He had sent Jesus all the way down to this world where people hit and killed each other, where people lied and betrayed each other. And this was the place where people lied about Jesus and betrayed Him. This was where people beat Him, and this was where Jesus said, "Baba, forgive them" before He died.

Nomi looked down again, and saw the lump of purple robes in the dirt beside her. "Miriam," she said, laying her hand on her friend's back. "Because of Jesus, I forgive you for what you did."

Miriam lifted her face, streaked with tears. Nomi saw

CHAPTER FOURTEEN

By the time they reached the hospital, Miriam was jabbering again. She told Peter about her plan to be a shopkeeper and drive her own car. He said he was going be an airplane pilot. The two of them made a plan in which Peter would fly all over Africa buying the bright fabrics and beautiful gowns Miriam would sell in her shop. They would both get very rich from this partnership. Miriam said she didn't mind driving Peter here and there in her car if he would fly her to Khartoum now and then to do her own shopping. He said he wouldn't mind flying her around, but she had to give him a new dress once a month for his wife.

Nomi could feel Peter looking at her, but she didn't return it. She didn't care about new dresses, because she was going be a teacher earning her own money and buying whatever she liked. And maybe she wouldn't marry Peter.

Who cared? She didn't. She was walking beside her two best friends on their way to see Grandmother. Nomi's heart and head and feet felt so light she thought she might be able to fly like that hawk. She would soar overhead—

A scream scattered her thoughts. Chills coursed through her as she halted, waiting for the sound of the guns.

"Nomi! Nomi! Nomi!"

But it was her mother instead, running toward her with both arms outstretched. Behind her, quickly overtaking his wife sprinted Baba. Her very own Baba. And there came Andrau. And behind him all the others, swarming around her, picking her up, hugging her, kissing her. Everyone wept, even Baba and Andrau. Then everyone laughed and talked all at once.

"Oh, Little Lamb!" Baba cried out, brushing tears from his eyes as he set her back on her feet. "We have searched and searched for you! We found each other in the forest, but no one knew where you went. We walked among the trees for many days, calling your name. And as we traveled to Uganda, we looked everywhere. And here you are! Right here!"

"I brought her to Uganda," Peter spoke up proudly. "I'm the one who found her in the forest and took her to the village of my Auntie and Uncle."

Nomi couldn't help but laugh at Peter's boasting. "It's true! Peter helped me a lot."

"Thank you, Peter," Mama said. "And, Nomi, you have a new home now. It's not far. We've been here several weeks, so our garden is already growing well. It's good soil here in Uganda, and this will be a fine place to live. A few days ago, we came to the hospital to visit Dorcas, and here we discovered Grandmother. And now you, our missing child!"

"How is Dorcas?" Nomi asked. Her sister had been shot in the leg and was not doing well when they all ran from the hiding place. "Is she better?"

"The doctors had to cut off her leg." Andrau spoke up for the first time. "But they told us she'll one day get a new one made of metal and plastic."

Despite the awful picture of Dorcas without her leg, everyone laughed over the idea of this new leg. Even Nomi chuckled. Whoever heard of such a thing? A plastic leg? These UNHCR people must have some strange ideas.

For the first time, Nomi took a moment to looked over the beloved faces of her happy family. Each one of them held a special place in her heart. Each one so dearly loved. But . . . but one was not here.

"Luke?" Nomi blurted out. "Where's Luke today?"

The laughter instantly stopped. Baba cleared his throat. "We don't know where Luke is. Not exactly. Andrau and I met someone who had seen him. Luke had gotten a gun, just as he said he would. But this person who saw him also noticed that the rebels had captured him."

Nomi's joy faded. "Is he dead?"

"Maybe not," Andrau told her. "Maybe he's alive."

"Alive - living as a soldier who has been forced to fight on behalf of the rebels," Nomi finished for her brother. "A child soldier."

"Or maybe he escaped," Mama said gently. "Maybe he's on his way to Uganda right now. Perhaps we'll find him standing at Grandmother's bedside when we go into the hospital. After all, that's where we found her."

"And you," Baba said. With one arm, he lifted Nomi high and kissed her cheek. "Now you have your family, and we have you."

With a last glance over her shoulder at Miriam and Peter, Nomi entered the hospital in her father's arms.

ABOUT THE AUTHOR

Catherine Palmer's first book was published in 1988, and since then she has published more than fifty books. Total sales of her books number more than one million copies.

Catherine's novels **The Happy Room** and **A Dangerous Silence** are ECPA best-sellers, and her Tyndale book A Touch of Betrayal won the 2001 Christy Award. She holds an undergraduate degree from Southwest Baptist University and a Master's Degree from Baylor University. Catherine and her husband, Tim, have two sons. They live in Atlanta, Georgia, where in addition to writing, Catherine is founder and director of the Refugee Sewing Society.

REFUGEE FRIEND DOLLS

Catherine Palmer founded the Refugee Sewing Society in 2008 in Metro Atlanta, Georgia, as a means by which refugee women from war-torn countries around the world could earn an income. Moved by the stories her ladies told, Catherine created the first in a series of Refugee Friend dolls.

This first doll, Nomi, represents refugees from Africa - specifically those from South Sudan. The accompanying book, **Nomi's Hiding Place**, tells the story of a twelve-year-old girl separated from her family when their village is attacked by rebel forces.

The Refugee Friend line will feature dolls and their books representing girls from Syria, Colombia, Bhutan, Congo, and other embattled nations around the world. Each doll will be sold wearing clothing native to her country. Additional clothing and accessories will be available. Each group of women at the Refugee Sewing Society participates in handcrafting all these items. They are eager for others to know their stories, after all!

Refugee Friend dolls, clothing and accessories are available at our online Etsy shop at etsy.com/people/refugeesewingsociety.

More information about the Refugee Sewing Society may be found at refugeesewingsociety.com.